Love, Masks, & Social Distancing

Caroline Carter

Magpie Publishing

Copyright © 2020 by Caroline Carter.

All rights reserved. No part of this book may be reproduced or used in any manner without written permission of the copyright owner except for the use of quotations in a book review.

December 2019

Messages

Text from Martin

What time are you going to be home?
Martin
Read 3.24pm

> Not until around 7, work is so busy today xx
> Sam
> Read 3.25pm

Look we need to talk

This isn't working out.
Martin
Read 3.25pm

> What isn't working? The flat? Yeah, it's way too small! Maybe I can look into properties tonight xx
> Sam
> Read 3.27pm

No Sam. Us.

I'm moving my stuff out tonight.
Martin
Read 3.27pm

> Wait, what the fuck!
> Sam
> Read 3.28pm

Martin is Typing

I've met someone. Someone who loves my poetry and really gets it. You know.
Martin
Read 3.28pm

The University of London

Louise Thorn-bough
Personal Representative
Human Resources
The University of London
Senate House,
Bloomsbury,
London WC1E 7HU

Samantha Duffy
Data Administration
The University of London
Senate House,
Bloomsbury,
London WC1E 7HU

Dear Ms Duffy,

Late this afternoon we received quite a few complaints from your colleagues about your recent behaviour. People have reported disruption of the workplace environment, damage to University property and a few members of staff have expressed concern for their own physical safety.

We are aware that this is not typical behaviour on your behalf and have taken this into account. We are also mindful that mental health is a serious and important matter. Therefore we have decided against taking any legal action and will not be pressing charges for damage of property. Instead, we ask that you see our in-house psychologist

The health and safety of our employees are our top priority and will be terminating your contract with us immediately.

Please clear out your desk by the end of the day, and give your key card and ID to the front desk.

Louise Thorn-bough
Personal Representative
Human Resources

To: Sam.Duffy@aol.com

From: Richards.Sally@London.ac.uk

Subject: Recap on First Session

Hi Samantha,

It was lovely meeting with you this afternoon.

I am just emailing you a recap of our first therapy session to remind you of what was discussed and what is being required of you going forward.

I have let the University know of your compliance and our arrangement of this matter. They have agreed that this is the best way to go about things.

Don't forget that the daily diary entries are mandatory and will have to be sent through to me every week. Any evidence that you have not been complying with this will be informed to legal where further action will be taken.

Kind Regards,
Dr Sally Richards.

Journal of Sam Duffy

Day 1

How do I even fucking start!

First, my boyfriend of two years breaks up with me through text! TEXT! He was the one who wanted us to move halfway around the world to live in London. "Oh, Sam, it will be great! It will make us even stronger blah blah blah" - that mother fucker. All because he thinks he's an artist because he writes shitty poems, and New Zealand isn't the place where his artistic talents can truly be expressed. What a load of bull shit.

So what do I get for being a supportive girlfriend?? None existent savings, dumped and left for some random girl from his temp job and THEN I GET FIRED! FIRED!

I have never ever been fired. I am a polite and hardworking employee, only to be fired because..yeah I had a little yell, and yeah I might have broken my work computer and thrown some shit. But my god, can you blame me?!

This day could not get any worse. I am on an hour-long train ride to get to my shitty studio apartment (that can barely fit a bed it's that tiny), with my eyes so red and puffy from crying all day that I can barely see. I WISH I COULDN'T SEE! The little I can see out of my pufferfish eyes are 20 people starring at me with pity and whispering to each other. Oh god...

I can't even pay for my shitty rent by myself.

I thought he loved me.

OMG, I thought those damn poems - the ones that actually weren't half bad and fucking romantic were about me. But of course not! It was that office ~~bitch.~~

...she's probably not a bitch. It's not like she was the one who cheated. HE'S THE BITCH.

Now I'm here penniless, loveless, jobless and stuck writing this damn journal to help manage my 'anger' and 'improve my mental health'. I DON'T HAVE ANGER PROBLEMS. I just got angry once! ONCE.

4th December, 2020

Hello, my darling Samantha,

Your mother gave me your new address. How is it over in London? Did you ever think about living in Ireland. You know your Grandfather and I were born in Ireland? It would just mean the world to us if you lived there, even for a short wee visit. You know that's where your lovely red hair comes from.

Your mother also mentioned you have been living with your boyfriend, Martin. How is he? I hope he is about to propose. You know it's the gentlemanly thing to do, you two have been together so long. I can always send my ring up to you if he is tight on money. I would love to see my little one married! Let him know for me, will you dare?

Are you coming home for Christmas? I would love to see you.

Write back soon,

Ta ta for now,

Love,

Granny xx

Journal of Sam Duffy

Day 2

Don't have much to journal about today.

Martin's stuff is all cleared out. The flat feels really empty without it. Which is hard because the apartment is full just having a bed in it.

I cried all last night until I fell asleep. Didn't feel angry this morning - that is until I went to finally change out of my work clothes and the bastard took all of MY T-Shirts! I paid a lot for those! So yeah I'm back to being pissed off ~~so sue me~~!

Oh yeah, I got a letter from my Grandma this morning asking when I was getting married....got to admit that set me back a bit.

Recovery from break up... -50%

It's hard sleeping alone.

Journal of Sam Duffy

Day 3

The really great thing about my apartment - I don't have to get out of bed to open the fridge!

Also massive bonus I can see my neighbors cats roam around the backyard. Chubby wee British Short Haired cats. The fattest one I have called Mr Blue, the more timid cat Ms Blue. Made my day - kind of. Maybe I should get a cat?

Recovery form break up -40%

Journal of Sam Duffy

Day 4

I feel so alone in this apartment. Like I'm always waiting for Martin to get home.

Watching romantic movies helps, their voices and constant distraction helps me forget that it's just me now, alone in a foreign country with no friends.

I have this constant lump in my throat that I can't seem to clear. My stomach is an uneasy ball of knots that you would think would stop me from downing a pint of ice cream, but you would be wrong.

Right now I'm not even mad, I just miss him. I want his arms around me again, just lying next to me. To smell his cologne.

Break up recovery -80%

Journal of Sam Duffy

Day 5

Pictures of us are still up on all of his social media accounts. Maybe he doesn't want to say goodbye to us just yet?

I want to delete all of our pictures from my phone and accounts and change my relationship status to single, not because I want to, but because I want him to see it, to feel hurt - as sad as I feel. It's somehow worse knowing he is fine and happy with someone else, that he doesn't need to mourn what we had like the last 2 years were nothing.

I need to tell my sister about it, I know it will make me feel better but I just.. can't yet. I feel so embarrassed and pathetic. I'm the girl who spent all of her money to follow a guy overseas, just to get stranded and left like an unwanted pet. I don't want people to think about me in that way - not yet.

Break up recovery - ~~75%~~

Journal of Sam Duffy

Day 6

I had a shower today.
Put on a fresh top and sweatpants. Like a whole new woman!
Tomorrow I might even go outside - my snacks are getting low. Did you know delivery is like an extra 4 pounds!

I need wine and tissues,... and chocolate.

I've stopped crying. My eyes just tear up now when I think about it or him or my expensive t-shirts or getting fired. So you know, progress.

I've been trying to lure the next-door neighbors cats up to my window so I can stroke them. I'm three stories up, but they can climb, and there's a little ledge they can sit on. I think I can manage a wee pat if I half dive out of the window. Definitely possible.

Okay, it might sound the tiniest bit unsettling behaviour. But I assure you Dr Richards, I've thought about it. I thought long and hard, and I'm positive getting a cat would really help me, have a bit of companionship, chill out and destress - you know? Although my ability to actually own a cat is limited. I can't pay for rent - that's given due to my lack of employment, as you are aware. So I will have to at some point go back to New Zealand (you know when I'm not going to be on a 40hour flight crying). Thus I have ruled out adopting a cat. Therefore to solve my lack of cat companionship problem, I shall befriend the neighbour's cats.

All in all, a very responsible and mature decision on my part.

Shopping List
- Wine
- Tissues
- For one meals
- Chocolate
- Cat treats
- ~~Ice Cream~~ Ice Cream

Face-to-Face

10:00pm 11/12/19

Lexa Duffy | Online

Call Connecting

Heyyyyyyy...omg you look terrible
Lexa

> Oh, thanks!
> Sam

I'm sorry, but it's true. What happened?
Lexa

> Martin dumped me.
> Sam

No!
Lexa

> Yup. Over text.
> Sam

What a fucking pussy! After two years he breaks up with you in a text!!
Lexa

> Oh, it gets worse - he had already packed up all of his shit and everything and moved into some other girls flat.
> Sam

Holy shit! What girl?
Lexa

> A girl from work. Apparently, lovvveeess his poetry and "really gets him".
> Sam

Mmm, I didn't like him anyway.
Lexa

> You didn't? Why didn't you tell me?
> Sam

I don't know, you two didn't seem like meant-to-be. Just like, this is a dude you're dating right now type of thing.
Lexa

And you didn't think to tell me this before I moved halfway around the world with him!
Sam

Woah dude, chill. Don't get angry with me. We both know you wouldn't have listened if I did. You're so stubborn.
Lexa

Oh, thanks, Lex. Can you not tell mum about this? At least not right now anyway?
Sam

Sure. Why don't you want her to know though?
Lexa

Ah, she'll be weird about it. Either she will be like "that's what you get for chasing a man and giving up your own plans" or wayyy to pitying, and I can't deal with that right now.
Sam

Haha omg, I can just hear her now! She wouldn't be wrong - you did give up your plans, and chase a boy halfway around the world.
Lexa

Lexa, can you not! Don't you think I feel shit enough? Your meant to be cheering me up, not making me feel worse
Sam

Sorry, no your right, that was very mum of me. So when are you coming back home?
Lexa

I don't know. I have to ask mum for a loan to buy the tickets.
Sam

Wait, don't you have a job?
Lexa

Um first, temp work doesn't pay very well, second, I've only been here for six months and ...I got fired.
Sam

Woahhh touchy. I get it your poor.
Lexa

Wait did you say fired?
Lexa

Thank you! Um, I had a wee, tiny rage at work when Martin broke up with me. Anyway enough about me hows Uni?
Sam

Hahaha, you idiot! Hey at least now you have nothing tying you down in London, and you can hang out with me instead!
It's okay - I got an A+ for my assignment. But when I went to collect my painting from the assignment wall, someone had taken it!
Lexa

NO! Again! Omg, I loved that piece. Have you asked the Uni if they can check the cameras and see who the little art thief is?
That's two paintings this year they have stolen, that should have at least, been ever so graciously gifted, and humbly received by me. Argh, I can't get over this.
Sam

Haha, chill I can always make you something for your birthday. And no I haven't, like why bother, I got my A.
Lexa

Yes, at least they were nice enough to take your painting after you got it graded...
Sam

Exactly! And plus they don't steal anyone else's, which is like, they must have thought mine was the best.
Lexa

Argh, you're killing me. What if this person has a weird crush on you and it starts with stealing your art, then little bits of your personal belongings, until eventually none of that is good enough. He or she - has to have all of you!
Sam

Get out of it! You're just mad you didn't steal it first.
Girl, you need to get some sleep. What time is it over there?
Lexa

10.30pm, so not too late. Hey, want to see something?
Sam

Yes! What? Show me!
Lexa

Tada! I have two cats.
Sam

Awww cute!
Wait - Oh, Sam! What did you do? Dumby you're coming back to New Zealand soon. You can't just adopt two cats!
Lexa

> I haven't! Don't worry Jeeesh. I have just happened to have befriended them.
> Sam
>
> I swear! Don't give me that look!
> Sam
>
> They roam around outside my apartment building all the time, looking so bored and cold because their owner never lets them in. So I tried calling them over from my window for pats. At first, they wouldn't budge, then after a day, they would come to my window and just like nervously questioned if they should allow pats to happen.
> Sam
>
> That is when I got my idea! Cat treats! I lured them over to my window and gave them treats, and while they ate, I stroked them. It only took like two more days after that, and they have been jumping through my window for pats and treats!
> Sam

Sam! Hahaha, you are going crazy. You just stole someone's cats!
Lexa

> Hey now, they can leave when they want. They just happen to like my company.
> Sam

Mmmm they are very cute.
Look I won't tell mum about...well all of this, if you start taking care of yourself.
Lexa

> Okay okay.
> Sam

I meant it. Like shower daily, put on fresh clothes - that aren't PJ's, brush your hair, and get some fresh air - that isn't just to the supermarket.
Lexa

> You ask a lot... but, okay, I shall try.
> Sam

All right loser, I'm gonna have breakfast. Now get some sleep.
Lexa

Journal of Sam Duffy

Day 9

I have successfully befriended my next-door neighbour's cats. I even got to cuddle Mr Blue! He is so cute and chubby. At least the cats love me. All I gotta do now is ween them off the treats, so they learn to come in on their own.

I am running dangerously low on Romantic movies on Netflix. I have watched Sleepless In Seattle like ten times now - probably will watch it again today. It just speaks to me. Like what if Martin was my Walter all of this time?!
We worked really well together. We hardly ever fought! Like we made a good team (at least I thought we did). I mean I never got that whole 'breath-stopping', 'I-can't-imagine-my-life-without-him' type feelings, I just thought that was like Rom-Coms being all dramatic. But what if it's not? What if we all meant to find someone that we can't breathe around??
What if Martin being an absolute piece of shit, is a total blessing in disguise?!
I could have been Meg Ryan settling for Walter when her Sam Baldwin was just a car ride away?

Oh, that reminds me! Called my older sister today. It was nice. She still annoys me, but it was really nice telling someone else about it. Also, she mentioned she didn't think Martin was the one for me - which totally backs up my theory. Martin is definitely my Walter....hopefully.

Break up Recovery 20%

TO Do

- Shower
- Brush Hair
- Brush Teeth
- Laundry
- Clean the flat
- Go for a walk (to the park)
- Email Mum about flights

Bank Account

Balance -£200

Overdraft Available £300

Journal of Sam Duffy

Day 10

I am sure you would be glad to know Dr Richards, (or should I say Sally? (:) I have reached a real turning point recently. I am sure that we will both come to the conclusion shortly, that I won't be needing to continue these little therapeutic diary entries anymore.

Today I felt like a new person. Last night's realisations that Martin was of course not the man I was meant to be with, and the break up actually being a really good thing - has given me a clearer outlook and improved my mood.

This morning I showered and got ready for the day. I even cleaned my flat until I could eat off the floor! It has never been so damn clean! And then I went for a lovely walk to my neighbourhood park, got a coffee and sat and watched some squirrels.

Truly, Dr Richards, I thank you. Deeply I do. There is something special about this diary technique. I truly feel calm and new again!

Recovery from breakup 50%

Journal of Sam Duffy

Day 15

Holy shit holy shit! It's one week until fucking Christmas!! Which means only two weeks until my landlord kicks me out.

Ah, fuck!

I've literally been curled up in my bed, sleeping and eating for a whole two weeks! How did I not realise! It felt like a few days tops...oh god I gotta tell mum about Martin AND ask for a loan. She is going to be so pissed off.

To: Prof.Duffy@aol.com
From: Sam.Duffy@aol.com
Subject: Catch Up!

Hi Mum,

So something happened. And before you read any more, please, yes I know 'I should have known better' and all of that - but I really need you to hold off on the second degree for a wee bit.

Anyway, Martin and I have separated. In the form of which he is staying at his new…at his friend's place.

I also may have lost my job :/

Can I pretty please get a loan for a plane ticket home?? I PROMISE to pay you back!

Love your favourite offspring,
Little Sammy
xxxxxx

P.s. did I mention I really miss you?

To: Sam.Duffy@aol.com

From: Prof.Duffy@aol.com

Subject: Catch Up!

Darling,

Oh, I am so sorry to hear that! I thought Martin was such a nice man. Though you could always do better with those lovely high cheekbones of yours.

I miss you too, honey. Plane tickets are a no I am afraid. As much as I love you, I can't coddle you anymore. Your twenty-three now sweetheart, you have to be more responsible. Didn't I always tell you to have a small emergency fund set aside for moments like these? Really I wished you did listen to me every now and again.

I know this seems harsh, and will probably sting even more while you are going through a broken heart. Still I am a feminist, and I don't know if I could call myself that again if I let my own daughter be set back by a man. Honey, you spent so much time and effort going to London, why waste all of that just because Martin and yourself are no longer an item. Is Martin giving up excellent job opportunities, experience and lovely overseas travel that comes with living so close to Europe? I think not. So why should you give all of that up?

If you want to come home, you will have to manage on your own. I cannot condone this type of behaviour from one of my own daughters.

Love you more,
Mum xox

P.s. Please write your grandma back.

BritishAir

London → Auckland

Total price from
£2,129

Tues, 19th Dec 18:50 - 12:05   28h 15m   1 Stop
BritishAir, Air Malaysia   LHR-AKL   5 hr 15m KUL

1 Free Carry On   1 Checked On Bag

Bank Account

Balance -£205

Overdraft Available £295

Lufthansa Airways

London → Auckland

Total price from
£1,550

Tues, 19th Dec 18:50 - 12:05   38h 25m   2 Stop
Lufthansa Airways, Pacific Air   LCY-AKL   FRA, HKG

1 Free Carry On   1 Checked On Bag

Messages

Sam: Hey could I borrow like a couple grand? I swear I will pay you back!!

Lexa: Hahahahaha that's funny.

Sam: Not even say $3,100 aka £1,550???

Lexa: Who do you think I am? A Kardashian. Girl, I am a struggling artist living in an expensive city.

Sam: Fuckkkkkk

Lexa: lol why?

Sam: I sucked it up and finally asked mum for a loan for plane tickets, and she flat out denied me!! My own mother.

Lexa: omg what?

Sam: Yeah! I know! But apparently, it's another one of her feminist stances and valuable learning moments. Now I'm stranded penniless and about to be homeless!

Lexa: Oh lol yeah that sounds about right. But how is it a feminist thing?

Sam: Idk like why is Martin staying and I'm leaving.

Lexa: She has a point. Like girl, you did too many extra shifts at the supermarket during Uni just so you could move to London once you graduated. And now what? You're leaving because some dick broke up with you??

Sam: Did you forget the jobless and not being able to pay next month's rent part?

Lexa: Just ring the agency and find another temp position, and then go out and find a hot British boy.

Sam: It's not that simple! It's almost Christmas! People won't be hiring now, and the agencies are all probably on break. OMG, I'm going to be homeless.

Lexa: Hey, hey, it's going to be okay! They can't kick you out straight away legally. You will find something, London's a big city. You just gotta try and stop crying.

Sam: It's just...Why is this happening to me?...Like what's the point of trying anyway?

Lexa: You are just mourning your relationship - totally normal dude! You were just as excited about this move as well. Oh, and you definitely can't go back without seeing Ireland - granny will kill you.

Lexa: I think you should stay - you will be grateful you stayed after all this. Sometimes things have to be really shit before they get better. And this is one of those times.

Sam: No you're right. I gotta suck it up :(....Maybe in a few days.

Journal of Sam Duffy

Day 16

Oh god, I think I'm having a panic attack.

I can't get home! I'm stranded in a foreign country with no money, no one I know to help me and no government help or anything!. I'm trapped. I am literally trapped. Oh fuck I almost forgot how small this apartment is. Jesus, it's hard to breathe.

Martin no longer cares about me. And now not even my own mum cares.

Break up recovery -1000%

Your Close Friend was Tagged in a New Post

Sasha tagged Martin
Location: The Shoreditch Poetry Club, London.

"When he writes poetry for you!"

To: Sam.Duffy@aol.com

From: Richards.Sally@London.ac.uk

Subject: Recap on First Session

Hi Samantha,

Hope you're doing well.

I'm just checking in to let you know I didn't receive last weeks diary entries. Please make sure to send them over to me by the end of today.

As this is the first time this has happened, I have not informed the University. If it happens again, I will have to report any cooperation on your behalf.

Kind Regards,
Dr Sally Richards.

Journal of Sam Duffy

Day 21

I saw a post a few days ago of Martin and "Sasha" on Facebook. He was tagged in one of her posts. Oh, and the caption - completely confirmed THE POEMS HE READOUT TO ME weren't inspired by me or were for me, but to get my opinion on them. MOTHER FUCKER WROTE POETRY FOR HER WHILE GETTING ME TO CRITIQUE IT!!!!!

Yeah, not fucking okay at the moment. And I'm sorry to say, Dr Richards, pretty mad right now and have somewhat reverted in my 'recovery'.

Like how could I have been so stupid to have trusted - let alone dated an arsehole like him!????

In my rage and depression, I forgot to write. I haven't done much recently. Just sleeping.

Ohhhhhh I almost forgot! I stalked her page. Like any normal person, and she fucking gorgeous. I mean if it was someone uglier than me, than you know I could consolidate myself with 'maybe he has a sex addiction' or 'needed more sex than we were having' or 'is a black and white cheater'. And it's wayyyyy worse than just - oh she's gorgeous - she is an entirely different 'type' to me. In every single way! Let me explain: She is a girly girl, is 5ft5, wears high heels, curly black hair, dress size must be a 6 if not smaller, cup size B (aka the perfect - I can wear any low cut outfit and look hot without duct tape & not be considered slutty - sized boobs). And then there is me: tomboy, only wears flat boots and trainers, 5ft 10, Strawberry blonde straight hair, size 10, cup DD! COMPLETELY different. God, I wanna crawl up and die.

I mean being dumped for someone insanely attractive is shattering, but holy shit is it worse if he chooses someone that is nothing like you.
1. It's not that he just wants sex
2. Or that he was lured in by this sexy devil and will eventually regret thinking with his microscopic penis.

It means that he intentionally (or subconsciously whatever) chose someone who wasn't me, that wasn't anything like me, because he doesn't want me at all!

....Lex says I'm overthinking it...I hope I am, but it doesn't feel like it right now.

Journal of Sam Duffy

Day 22

It's Christmas...

To celebrate this festive day, I brought my two fluffy housemates a few cans of tuna. Splurged and got myself the nicest supermarket Prosecco I could find (only £11!). I think the pairing goes quite nicely with a care package of New Zealand snacks. Of course, chips and Prosecco go beautifully together, but you must try it with a few drops of your own salty tears, one hand trying to drink while the other angrily tries to unwrap the individual Christmas chocolates. Such fun!

God this tv show Miranda is hilarious. I'm quite tipsy, I've blasted the heating so it's about two hundred degrees in here and I fucking refuse to take off my Christmas socks and jumper. Otherwise, I'm just a sad girl crying into her chocolate. This way I'm a sad girl on Christmas crying into her chocolate.

Anyway Merry Christmas Dr Richards.

P.s why is it not fucking snowing, was 'Love Actually' a complete lie??

Journal of Sam Duffy

Day 23

Omg, I had a bloody heart attack this morning. While both of the cats jumped through my window (on their own accord!), the neighbour across from me yelled up from his tiny ass garden. My poor heart! I was only wearing an oversized t-shirt - no bra! Like he could have seen my undies or my non-existent pale ass bum!

Anyway, he yelled up at me "Hey! I think my cats have adopted you!". I replied in complete and utter shock "oh god yeah sorry! I keep the window open, so they come and go when they like. I can keep them out if you want?". He said very nicely - except I know it wasn't actually meant to be that nice because I could see his wife glaring at me through their wall-length sliding doors - "That's fine! Just make sure not to feed them or they will get even fatter.". Which I replied with "haha yeah they are a bit tubby, won't feed them I promise!"

God that was so humiliating like I've already stopped feeding their cats. They come over to me because they want to. I can't help that they love me more. Plus the wife doesn't even let them inside!

I SWEAR I DID NOT STEAL THEIR CATs.

Messages

Text from Don't Answer

How are you doing?

Don't Answer

Read 1.25pm

Do you need any money to get back to NZ? I'm happy to loan you some

Don't Answer

Read 1.30pm

Come on Sam, I feel bad

Don't Answer

Read 1.50pm

To: John@HammerRecruitment.com

From: Sam.Duffy@aol.com

Subject: Any Jobs Available

Hi John,

I was wondering if you had any temp jobs, preferably starting as soon as possible?

Cheers,
Sam.

To: Sam.Duffy@aol.com

From: John@HammerRecruitment.com

Subject: Any Jobs Available

Hi Sam,

It's been a while! Sorry to hear about what happened with the University position. Surprised you didn't contact me earlier!

We have a few positions available, but they won't start until February. Will this be okay?

- John.

To: John@HammerRecruitment.com

From: Sam.Duffy@aol.com

Subject: Any Jobs Available

Ahh February is a bit too far away. Is there nothing that I can take sooner than that? I need to pay rent. I will take anything!!

To: Sam.Duffy@aol.com

From: John@HammerRecruitment.com

Subject: Any Jobs Available

I have a job that would actually be the perfect fit for you. But there is some good and bad news.

Bad news first: It's based outside of London, in Brighton, which is out in East Sussex.

Good news: Relocation package so next months rent will be all sorted, it's a beach town, oh and it's not in London.

Start date would be January. Let me know!

Search: Brighton, UK

Visiting Brighton

Brighton is a popular tourist location. The beachside city, is renowned for its diverse communities, quirky shopping areas, large and vibrant cultural, music and arts scene and its large LGBT population, leading to its recognition as the "unofficial gay capital of the UK".

To: John@HammerRecruitment.com

From: Sam.Duffy@aol.com

Subject: Any Jobs Available

I will take it! :)

To: Anderson@GamingCo.com

From: John@HammerRecruitment.com

Subject: Found the perfect employee for you

Andy!

Mate, I have found the perfect person to fill that position of yours.

Fast Details: Hardworking, University Educated, loves video games, and is female (I know how much you've wanted to increase your diversity hires).

Let me take you out for a pint tonight at The Pond, and we can talk properly then.

- John.

PearTree

Property X Brighton & Hove X

Spacious Room Available! All Bills Included £650pm

2 Bedroom in The Lanes!

Current Flatmates: A couple. 1 female, 1 male. Australian/British. Working Professionals. Really laid back, love to have a pint at the pub, or a quiet night in.

PearTree

Spacious Room Available! All Bills Included £650pm

Hi, I was wondering if the room is still available? I would love to view it sometime!
A little bit about me, I recently moved to the UK from New Zealand, have spent the last 6 months in London and thought moving to Brighton would be just a bit of fresh air I need (literally haha). I am 23, just got a job in Brighton as a Q/A game tester. I am quite laid back and easy going, clean and totally pay my rent on time :)

Sam, Seen

Hey girl,
Omg, you're from New Zealand - I'm from Aus! We're basically country cousins! Yes, totally! Come view the flat whenever!

Mia, Seen

Face-to-Face

11:02pm 27/12/19

Lexa Duffy | Online

Call Connecting

Hey Loser
Lexa

> I got great news!
> Sam

Oh yay! Did mum give up and get you a ticket home?
Lexa

> I mean..it's not that good. But I got this fucking text from Martin asking if I needed money to get home! He actually assumes I'm moving back! AND that I need his help like as if.
> Sam

Oh my god, he did not! To be fair though both those assumptions are correct - you do want to go home AND need financial help.
Lexa

> Lexa, what fucking side are you on?
> Sam

Argh, I'm sorry it's true! It doesn't take away from the fact that he's a dickhead. Anyway, what's the good news?
Lexa

> God I don't even want to tell you anymore.
> Sam

Come on! I'm sorryyy
Lexa

> Okay well I decided fuck Martin, and to show him I can still have a great fucking time over here without him so I contacted my recruitment agent, and he got me a job!!
>
> — Sam

That's such great news - now you can pay rent!
Lexa

> That's not just it though. It's in Brighton - it's like a really cool beach town, AND the job is at a game studio, AND they are offering to pay me to relocate which covers first months rent and bond!
>
> — Sam

Holy shit! You are actually soo lucky. Though I thought the plan and whole reason you moved to the UK is for the London experience and lifestyle or whatever.
Lexa

> Well yeahhh but you know, I've had six months of living in London, and I definitely need a fresh start right now. Like fuck Martin. Next year, I will be in a cool UK city, super thin, successful, dating a super hot British surfer. Like it will be so good I can feel it.
>
> — Sam

Totally, like you definitely need to get out of this funk! And being in a different mindset will allow you to stop thinking about that arsehole 24/7 like you are at the moment...I mean it's kinda sad and like I love you but you look a damn mess.
Lexa

> ......just because you have never had your heartbroken. IT'S SHIT LEX!
>
> — Sam

Omg touchy, okay I guess it's bad, but man I thought you were showering.
Lexa

> I have been! Recently.
>
> — Sam

Did you wash your hair? Change your clothes? Drink anything other than wine?
Lexa

Hey all of my tops and jumpers were taken by Martin, and it's too cold to wear anything but sweatpants and a hoodie.
Sam

What! He took your clothes? Whyyyyyyy
Lexa

Ahh well, coz technically they are guys clothes, but I was so sick of wearing tops and jumpers with like butterflies and shit on it and guys clothing is SO much cooler. Plus with us having to fit our whole life into a suitcase we thought it would be a good idea to have like unisex stuff so we could share - you know??
Sam

Oh yeah! Guys clothes are cool. Omg you can get a whole new wardrobe and get like a damn post break up glow up! I've always wanted to do one of those, but like…I've never had one.
Lexa

Oh my god. I'm signing off now. I just can't.
Sam

Journal of Sam Duffy

Day 25

I feel a change in the air!

1. I got a new job
2. I'm being a damn strong independent woman and deciding not to run home to mum and stick it out here, in the United Damn Kingdom.
3. I am moving cities to a beautiful beach town where I will be independent and financially stable!

I don't need no damn man!

I'm gonna make next year my bitch!

<u>2020 year of perfect vision!!!!!!!</u>

The only thing is, I'm going to miss Mr and Ms Blue SO MUCH. Like how am I going to be able to lure someone else cats into loving me in Brighton?? :(

Journal of Sam Duffy

Day 26

I need to stop stalking Martin and his new 'girlfriend', 'Sasha'.

She's middle-classed, loves her family's horses, all out in town with her 'girls', never EVER would dreammm of missing a spin or yoga class. Where does she find the time?? Like I know she has a job, and apparently friends...she seems to have so many more hours in the day to me...like who is she - Beyonce?

I even got to the point where I was stalking her exes...

......I really gotta stop.

Journal of Sam Duffy

Day 27

It's the eve of a new year, a new chapter!
No fuck boys, no crying.
A new age of feminine wiles, sexual freedom, hot British boys, cocktails, beach walks, and maybe even learning how to skateboard??

I'm nervous as fuck doing anything alone and christ moving cities in a foreign country……actually no! Every girl in their twenties needs to do this. Be single, go overseas and taking risks! Omg like if I didn't come here, I could have been married and stuck with small dick energy Martin forever!!!! Your twenties are for risks, sex and doing crazy shit to brag about when you're in your 80's when you can't walk.

Though Lexa was right, I look like a fucking cavewoman right now. I need to get my shit together. It's gonna be difficult with non-existent money, but I will at least shower, straighten my hair and shave…oh god my poor razor. I'm gonna have to add that to my shopping list.

I can't wait for my first pay to do the full glow up!

Journal of Sam Duffy

The look good, feel good To-Do List

- Shower
- Wash hair
- Shave EVERYWHERE
- Straighten Hair
- Pluck monobrow
- Wax upper lip
- Makeup
- Laundry
- Put on jeans
- Cut and paint nails

January 2020

Journal of Sam Duffy

Day 29

The year of Sam is finally upon us!!!!!
It's going to be such a fucking good year - I can feel it in my bones.

I've packed up all of my shitty belongings into a gym bag and big red suitcase! Ready to move to Brighton and into my new Flat!!!!
I mean the suitcase wheels don't technically work and I was red and sweaty from lugging it on to like 4 different trains, and lots of people stared, but that doesn't matter because it's a fresh start! And in no way a sign of how this year is going to go.

I am currently on the Express train direct to Gatwick Airport and Brighton, so I have enough time to plan out the year, write my resolutions and need to do's. Fuck I LOVE a list.

Break up recovery - 150%

Journal of Sam Duffy

2020 Resolution

Never ever again stalk Martin or his new GF!

Also, I promise to live like a damn thriving twenty old, letting loose and living her damn life - not some sad bitch.

2020 Goals

- Expel Martin from my life!
- Save enough money to travel.
- Travel to Paris, Morocco, Ireland, Scotland, Italy, Greece, Croatia, the Netherlands.
- Listen to Feminist Podcasts.
- Loose 5 kgs
- Become hot aka GLOW UP
- Get a hot new boyfriend.
- Read Feminist Lit
- If it's less than an hour away - walk (aka stop being a lazy bitch).
- Go to flat parties and clubs on the Beach.
- Learn how to surf or/& Skateboard
- Pride Week/Carnival Brighton!!!!

Achieve Goals To-Do List (now)

- Block Marlin on everything
- Take down all of pics of us together.
- Delete pictures from phone and burn all items he has given me or reminds me of the small-dicked prick.
- Hunt down a great feminist podcast or two
- Maybe watch some youtube videos on how to save.

Achieve Goals To-Do List (when I get paid)

- Join a gym
- Buy new clothes
- Hair cut and dye
- Nails professionally done.
- Buy new makeup
- Buy a pushup bra and body contour
- Buy some feminist literature
- Get a Tinder Account
- Go club/pub/cocktail bar whatever they have
- Sign up for surfing lessons
- Buy a longboard

To: Sam.Duffy@aol.com

From: **anderson@GamingCo.com**

Subject: First Day

Heya Samantha,

We are so happy you will join our small GamingCo family next Monday!

I just wanted to chuck you a quick email reminding you that you won't need to bring a laptop with you or anything like that as we have everything sorted.

Paydays are monthly. We have drinks as a team on Fridays and free office lunches!

If you need any advice on Brighton or any suggestions on what to go see and explore, I would be delighted to help out.

- A.

Messages

Text from Mia (new flatmate)

Hey Girl! Let me know when you get in, me and Parker will meet you at the station to help carry your bags and let you into the building xx

Mia
Read 11.12am

Omg that's wayyy to nice, but really I'll be okay!

Sam
Read 11.12am

Girl don't be silly! I still remember how painful it was training in with all of our bags and getting it into our flat when we first moved to Brighton and there were two of us!

Mia
Read 11.15am

Anyway, Parker will be the one carrying the heavy stuff xx

Mia
Read 11.15am

Haha thank you SO much! My train is about 5mins away from the station now. I'll see you soon x

Sam
Read 11.30am

Face-to-Face

10:45pm 01/01/20

Lexa Duffy | Online

Call Connecting

Finally! I was wondering when you were gonna call - now show me the new flat, please!
Lexa

Okay Okay, give me a second.
So it's still quite messy coz I haven't quite unpacked yet, but this is my room.
Sam

OMG! It's basically the size of your London apartment.
Lexa

I know! And wait until you see the lounge and kitchen.
Sam

Heyy wait a minute is that my fucking dress?
Lexa

Um anyway over here...
Sam

Sam, I've been looking for that everywhere!
Lexa

Ahh, whoops!
Sam

You're so lucky your like 40 hours away
Lexa

Anyway, this is the hall and in there is where Mia and here Boyfriend Parker sleep. They have such a cool bedroom - which is a little bit bigger but is totally fair coz there is two of them.
Sam

Nice. Now show me the lounge.
Lexa

Okay, it's just through here. TA DA!
Sam

Dammmn you have an L couch and a fucking kitchen island. This place is so nice! Why didn't you move here earlier?
Lexa

I know right, AND it's only like £50 more expensive than my old place in London, and it includes bills.
Sam

Oh, I'm so jealous. Do you have a balcony?
Lexa

Not really - I mean kinda, you can open this like window/door and then shimmy your way across the ledge.
Sam

Hey, I would call that a balcony! Technically you're outside and you have support rallying. You should have coffee out there!
Lexa

Ahhh yes! Ekk this place makes me so happy already! And I'm right in The Lanes which is so fucking cool and like trendy - I only ever see people in their twenties walking around here, well except the tourists.
Sam

Omg, can I come to visit you!
Lexa

Yes! I would love that!
Sam

Yay, it's a plan! I could probably save up and come by April!
Also, where are your flatmates?
Lexa

Oh they're out with some friends at a pub, they asked me to come along, but I am so exhausted, and I still need to unpack!
Sam

That's nice of them!
Lexa

Yeah, they even helped me get my heavy ass bags to the flat from the station. Like I love them already!
Sam

awww I'm so jealous right now. I barely see my flatmates, sometimes I wonder if I'm the only one that lives here.
Lexa

haha remember when I came to visit you, and one of them basically ran away back into their room whenever I went into the lounge?
Sam

haha omg yeah I think that was Toby!
Lexa

How's everything? Anything new with you?
Sam

Well...yes actually!

Lexa

Omg, what? Tell me!

Sam

I think I have a boyfriend?

Lexa

A BOYFRIEND! Holy shit, you didn't even tell me your were seeing someone...

Sam

I know I know, but you and Martin had literally just broken up, and i could not have told you then.

Lexa

...fair. Okay out with it, woman! I need the details - All of them!

Sam

Okkkkaaay so he is really cute and tall and loves like the outdoors and stuff.

Lexa

Ah ha keep going.

Sam

Um well, we met online lol. He is super nice, a web developer....And he is a little bit older than me...

Lexa

27? oh, do you mean like 40's?

Sam

No! Not middle-aged god. He's 31...
Lexa

Oh, Lex that's not that old! What have I always told you, you have to date someone older. They are way more mature, know what they want in life and aren't still in that bro/partying phase.
Sam

Haha you are so right! I like really like him.
Lexa

Aw, I'm so happy for you! I can't wait to meet this guy.
Sam

Well, I don't know if we will get to that yet - still too early to do the whole meet my family thing.
Lexa

Are you blushing! You want to kissss him! -
Sam

Ew stop
Lexa

- You want to marry him! -
Sam

Haha omg, get out of it! I will hang up on you!
Lexa

- you want to have his babies.
Sam

Call Ended

Journal of Sam Duffy

Day 30

Waking up in this apartment is so nice!!
I had my morning coffee out on our tiny balcony and I just people watched as they walked by the shops below us. The people here seem so much more relaxed than in London. It's nice.

When I eventually came inside, Mia rushed out of her bedroom, her braided hair flying behind her, with big fluffy socks on wooden floors. She almost smashed right into me!
She told me about this new years event they are having down at the beach tonight and that I had to come with her.
I agreed straight away - like straight away. If Mia wasn't so excited about the party, she would have been weirded out by how desperate I am for 1. a friend, and 2. alcohol...and boys (so 3).

Anyway It's perfect the only friends I made from uni was when I was drunk and that includes boyfriends. I'm so shy and overthink everything when I'm sober that when I drink, I'm like this beautiful social butterfly. Yes! This is going to be great!

Though there is one wee snag. I have nothing to wear!!!

I don't know how it happened, but I gained like 5kgs in this past month! So now that's like 10kgs I have to lose before I look like a damn Victoria Secret model and make Martin cry.

And you know how I found out I gained all of that weight??! I finally got into something other than sweatpants and tried on an old dress, which I couldn't zip up! My boobs were almost con-caved, restricting my bloody airways trying to close it.

I'm not gonna lie I did tear up about it. Thank fuck for concealer.

Also, I know I know Dr Richards, being ultra-thin is like this made-up construct from the beauty industry, selling this unobtainable standard of beauty so that you think you can achieve it by buying their products. But I just got cheated on so stop with the guilt trip Dr Richards, I need a little ego boost, not a huge lofty downer.

It's worse because Mia is like this tall brown-skinned goddess who could wear anything and she looks like Naomi Campbell :(

I went from being a damn snack to looking like I ate all the snacks! .....Which I fucking did.

Just a potato girl on New Years.

Journal of Sam Duffy

Day 32

About the other night. My god! What even happened?

These are the things I know:
Mia got upset because Parker had to stay home and forfeit drinking because he had to go into work the next day. Hence she decided to remedy this by making us play a drinking game.
Then we went out for drinks at the pub so she could practise her Wing-Woman position. Which didn't go well because as soon as they saw her and then a sad bitch drinking alone in a booth, I was not surprised when their interest laid elsewhere.
That's when she decided I needed to cheer up and get my head into it, so she brought us shots.
I remember us on the beach, I think I was making out with someone, but I can't remember who.

And that's it.
All in all, a very very fun night.
I'm pretty sure Mia and I are best friends now.

Oh god but I couldn't move yesterday, I was so hungover. I couldn't even turn on the light, my head was thumping so badly.

I'm still not feeling 100%.

Journal of Sam Duffy

Day 34

Today Mia and I had a girls day. We baked cinnamon rolls, half with extra caramelised filling over the top, and the other half with cream cheese icing. Not a fan of cream cheese so we compromised. And then we ate them watching The Princess Bride while doing our nails and wearing face masks.

I think Mia is just as lonely as I am. She met her boyfriend Parker at the University of Victoria, over in Australia. They've been together for almost 5 years! Anyway, I digress. They moved to London so he can earn more money to take back to Australia for when they want to settle and have kids. Which is SO cute! Parker got a job in this finance law firm thing (I have no idea what she said his job was, I just pretended I knew), in Brighton and had to train in from London every day. So they decided to move to Brighton so he wouldn't have to spend like 4 hours every day on the train. That is one thing I love about Brighton - being able to walk everywhere, man I did not enjoy the trains! Cramped, late and expensive.

Oh god sorry, I keep rambling! Anywayyy, yeah, so like me she has moved here for a boy, living in a city where she has no friends. I mean it's pretty cool she works as a barista in the UK and then goes home and writes her screenplay, but she is basically all by herself because even though Parker saves heaps of money, he's never here and when he is, Parker is so stressed out he gets stoned and just blobs.

I feel for Mia. I'm glad though I have someone in a similar situation as I am. Thank god I moved to Brighton!

...oh yeah what the hell is happening in China?

Journal of Sam Duffy

Day 35

Today is my first day of work at Gaming & Co. I am so nervous. I woke up like 10 times last night, checking my phone to see if I had slept in. Until finally, I just got up at 6am.

I straightened my hair, my make up took an hour, but it's perfect. I showered, brushed my teeth, ate breakfast, had coffee. Literally have done everything but I still feel so fucking nervous. I don't know why, but I feel like I'm forgetting something?

The place is technically in Hove, which is only about 30-45min walk tops. But I've lived in London for half a year, so that sounds amazing! It's basically the same amount of time it took me to train into my old job.

Wish me luck!

Journal of Sam Duffy

Day 36

Okay so I spent like an hour and a half doing my makeup and hair to look amazing for my first day yesterday and what happened?! I sweated it off.

45mins walk is actually a lot if your unfit and usually take the train. I was literally fast walking like that guy off Kath and Kim. I was nervous about being late, so I had to quicken my pace a bit. Turns out I was very early, but I had basically sweated off all of my foundation, and my hair went super frizzy! So, I was in the toilet wiping off the sweat and foundation, with my hair now slicked back into a pony by sweat, wiping my cleavage dry, panting hoping no one would notice.

And that's not even it! Nerves + wayy too much coffee + a 40min jog, and I damn near destroyed the toilet on my first day. Thank god no one went in there after me. Like oh my god.

Besides all of that - everyone was so welcoming and so lovely! They had even heard of New Zealand, like either you are really into Lord of The Rings or a geography major, and even then NZ isn't put on every map because it's so small people just forget. Omg so sorry Mrs. Richard! I really need to stop rambling.

My boss and my other boss, a female/male duo of badass game studio owners. I loved seeing a female as a director of a game studio - an industry mostly dominated by males.
Actually, I was like the second female employee there, apart from my boss...

It's such a cool job! I just get to play their upcoming games all day and write about fixes or bugs that need to be made!

If Martin found out, he would be so fucking jealous!

But this isn't about him. This is about me and how I enjoy my new job. Because I am now fully over that boy and don't even think about him while I am living such a cool and more improved life!

7th January, 2020

Dear Grandma,

Thank you so much for your last letter, I loved it! I wish I could have been with you for Christmas, but the flights were far out of my price range.

I'm no longer living in London, as I have found a really great job in Brighton, UK. I will add my new address on the back of the letter for you granny.

Martin and I are doing well, and yes, I will let him know for you! I can't wait to go to Ireland, don't you worry granny - it is top of my list. I just have to save a little bit first. I will send you pictures of my trip to Ireland when I go :)

Hope you are doing well, and Auntie Claudia isn't annoying you too much!

Love,
Your Favourite Grandchild,
Samantha
xoxo

Journal of Sam Duffy

Day 39

I know I decided to walk to and from work every day instead of catching the bus because well I have no money and am literally just eating toast and baked beans, but also to help lose weight while I don't have money for a gym membership —- But I hate it!

I'm so lazy. Like why try to make myself into something that I am not? Do I want to be fit? Yes. Do I want to exercise? Absolutely not.

I should have taken Martin's offer on the loan and asked for 2 grand. Buggered off to Brighton, bought myself a bus pass, and a gym membership and then never pay it back or talked to him again. That fucking dick. He would have totally deserved it.

I feel like girls should get financially compensated when shit like this happens.

Costs to Cover:
- Emotional damage
- Loss of confidence and self-worth
- Financial loss of weeks stuck in bed
- Dwindling sense of trust in men
- Inconvenience fees

Messages

Text from Mia (new flatmate)

Girl, we NEED to go out tonight!
Mia
Read 5.05pm

Ah, I don't know M, I'm pretty tired from work.
Sam
Read 5.15pm

How are you ever gonna find yourself a hot British man if I can't take you out? Plus Parker is free tonight, so he's shouting drinks!!
Mia
Read 5.16pm

You are so damn wise. Okay, I will come!
Sam
Read 5.23pm

Sweet!! I will get us all done up, so don't you worry. M has everything covered. Drinks at the Twisted Lemon?
Mia
Read 5.23pm

Sounds fucking perfect x
Sam
Read 5.25pm

Journal of Sam Duffy

Day 47

I'm happy to say I have gone almost a whole month without stalking Martin or his new GF. I barely even think about him anymore!

2020 is already the year of Sam, and it's barely February.

Last night Mia, Parker and I went out for cocktails - it was so much fun! I'm so glad to have them as flatmates. And watching those two together just reminds me how wrong Martin and I were for each other! They have been together for 5 years, and the way he looks at her is so adorable. He just doesn't realise anyone is around when he is with her. Whenever she talks, Parker just looks so proud and mesmerised by her. Even their conversations, they don't just talk, they have deep conversations, lightly debate things and tease each other constantly. It's like.....watching an old married couple who been together 40 years and still adore each other.

It makes me a little bit sad. Not in a 'missing Martin' type of way but in a, 'I wish I had this', 'I hope I find someone like this', type of sadness if you get what I mean??

Anyway, so last night after a few cocktails outside, I went back into the crowded bar (and when I say crowded I mean, people pressing on you crowded). I was standing close to the bar trying to order another round of drinks, when this guy turns around and smirks at me. Like a young Johnny Depp, knees going mush type of smile. Oh boy, did I fucking blush. I HAD to look away! He was wayyyy too hot. And then he calls out to me saying "if your ordering for your friends, it's going to be a long wait'.

Omg his voice! He sounded like Colin Farrell! It was at that exact moment if he didn't leave me alone, I would have jumped him. I have no idea what I said to him, and neither did he. After those cocktails, my voice was basically gone. I remember he laughed and then as the bartender passed him his round of drinks, he gave them to me! Saying 'You have them, my friends are too buggered to remember drinking them anyway" and then he gave me that smile again. I'm not proud of it, but It took me a good minute to muster up a horse reply of "What about your friends? Or did you just order these in hopes of attracting a desperate young lass?". I fucking said 'Lass' in an IRISH accent. WHAT HAS HAPPENED TO ME. I've somehow lost all ability to flirt let alone interact with someone from the opposite sex. SO fucking embarrassing. Thank god he laughed otherwise I would have crawled home.

He was like "I wish that's what I was doing instead of buying those idiots drinks, so I guess in a way I am buying drinks for some Lasses, just not in the way I would have hoped". He was so witty, like what the fuck. Usually, guys can't keep up, but here I was barely able to form a sentence, and there is this beautiful, funny, Irish man. I collected the drinks thanking him, thinking like damn that was a smooth pick up on his end, and went back to my friends. I thought he would try find me and flirt some more, but nope. Didn't see him.

I tried going back to the bar to see if he would be there, but he was nowhere to be seen.

Now that I think back on it, I should have asked him to help me carry them back to my friends, instead of some socially crippled girl trying awkwardly to carry three cocktails back outside in a crowded bar while trying to look confident and alluring.

God damn, I need to get my game back. Maybe I need to go to like speed dating, like practise rounds of flirting.

I told Mia and Patrick about it, and they laughed at me!

So a good night out, but a cringe moment I will remember forever and will haunt my fucking dreams.

Journal of Sam Duffy

Day 54

Life in Brighton update
- Work is great!
- I'm still walking to work!
- Lost 3kgs of the breakup weight!
- Will be paid in 5 days!!! aka 120 hours aka four sleeps away

Sundays have become Mia and I's tradition to go out and buy ingredients for Sunday Baking. In which we eat said baking while watching chick flicks and putting on face masks.

It's the highlight of my week; otherwise, I'm - sweaty walking to work, working, getting home and falling straight to sleep.

I told M that I wasn't looking forward to my Birthday next month. I had always wanted to go to Paris, Martin and I planned on going this year. Doing it alone just seemed sad and lonely, and not going to Paris for my Birthday seems just as bad. M decided her and Parker were going to take me. I would have said no because I hate third-wheeling - especially a pity third wheel. But when I hang out with them, it's like we've all been friends for the longest time. And she seemed genuinely so excited about the idea, so I agreed!

Birthday in Paris…alone but still, maybe I will find a cute French boy??

Also, I was reading the news in 'The London Times', and apparently someone came in from China and has infected like five people with a virus. I wonder if it's like Swine Flu?

So many people were really worried, but it went away quite fast... though I can't remember most of it because I was like 12.

Journal of Sam Duffy

Day 59

PAYDAY BITCHES!!!!

Omg, I was so excited this morning I did a little dance.

I can't wait not to have to eat toast for each meal and to be bought drinks by my wayyyyy too lovely flatmate.

I know I don't get paid until 5pm tonight, but I have already gone ahead and booked everything to set myself up for a ME fucking day! I deserve it for fuck sake.

Tomorrow aka Saturday, aka glow-up/pamper day. I have booked myself in for a hair cut and balayage at 9am at 'The Lanes' hairdressers (it sounds early but I am not even going to be able to sleep - it feels like Christmas!). Then I have a manicure booked for 12pm. Then I'm going to treat Mia and get us to brunch and go thrift/vintage clothes shopping. Then we are going to get me some proper skincare and makeup so I can get ready for drinks at the Twisted Lemon Cocktail bar later that night where of course I will be shouting them! Eeekkkk I am so bloody excited.

Year of Sam 2020!!!

February 2020

Journal of Sam Duffy

Day 61

Fuuuuckkkk why does everything have to be in sterling pounds :(

I woke up this morning from a great night out to a notification from my bank saying I've already gone over my month's budget!

I HAVE to get a gym membership! Even if I can't put money into an emergency fund or travel....oh, shit Paris....Okayyy, I will just ~~make sure not to buy any takeaway coffee~~ eat toast. That's not that bad - at least I will be back to my pre-breakup weight before I meet all the French boys!

Why do you have to get paid monthly here???? I can barely budget properly when getting paid weekly.

Budget
- Only buy 3 coffees per week
- Weekly grocery shopping £20
- Try to find a gym membership under £40
- Buy cheap (I mean dirt cheap tickets to Paris)

Ryan Air

London → Paris, France

Total price from
£30

Fri, 7th Feb   19:00 - 20:05   1hr   0 Stops
Ryan Air   LGW-PAR

1 Free Carry On   0 Checked On Bags

Ibis Paris Avenue de la République

Standard Double Room
Max persons: 2

1 double bed

1 night, 1 adult

£90
Feb 7–9

4.0 Stars

Bright rooms in a modern budget hotel offering a stylish bar, a contemporary lounge & free Wi-Fi.

Journal of Sam Duffy

Day 62

Today is the first Monday of February, the start of a new month and a new week! I am ready to take my soon to be modelesque butt to the gym!

I've woken up early, at 6am so I can get there before anyone else and be in the gym training, then shower and head off to work!

This is going to be so good. I can't wait until Martin sees the new me and cries stupid little tears. I'M SO PUMPED! I've got my rage workout playlist, that I spent all of last night curating ready to go!

I found this gym like 5mins away from me for only £39 a month! I LOVE living in The Lanes. Also since Mia and I are both super bummed that I couldn't join her fancy-ass gym (it's like £20 per class??!!), she gets a free buddy pass once a week, so I can still go with her to Prossecco Friday Spin class!! I love 2020 already!

Journal of Sam Duffy

Day 63

I am sooooooo sore holy shit. I can barely move. I might have to bus home (but definitely cannot let it be a daily thing!).

On the plus side the rage playlist worked a damn treat, every time I felt too lazy or got too tired I just switched songs and I was back to seeing Martin's stupid face when he read his poetry!

The downside is that there is like 3 flights I have to go up to get to work (as they have no elevator - can you believe that?) and 2 flights ups to my my apartment because our elevator will never be fixed.

Also I know it's only been a day but I swear I could already see a difference in my bum in the mirror this morning...it definitely looked more toned.

As the French say 'it has to hurt to be beautiful' or something like that. If that's true, I must look like the queen of the fucking ball right now!

p.s why does everyone in Brighton go to the gym so early? I mean you're meant to have given up your new years resolutions by now?? ALSO, why do they all look like influencers? Not even regular influencers, but the gym buff influencers. It should be against gym policy.

Messages

Text from M

2 days until PARIS!!!
M
Read 10.25am

> EKKK I AM SO EXCITED
> Sam
> Read 10.26am

Girl, you will LOVEEE it! I can't wait to show you around and take you out on the town!
M
Read 10.30am

> Yes! All the French boys! You and parker have to be my wing people!
> Sam
> Read 10.31am

Well, of course girl!… I don't know much french but I'm sure I can think of something ;)
Also speaking of being a great wing woman. Wanna use my weekly free 'bring your friend' gym pass to come to box fit with me tonight?
Since we can't go to Prossecco and Spin on Friday because we'll be in PARIS!
M
Read 10.35am

> Ahhh…no because I am lazy and my body says 'please god no'.
> …but I will be there at 6pm because I want to eat pastry in France :) x
> Sam
> Read 10.37am

Lol yay xx
M
Read 10.41am

Journal of Sam Duffy

Day 67

Paris Baby!!

Okay so lesson learned - Ryan Air flights are fucking cheap, but my goodness do not fly with them! Most importantly I got to Paris at midnight instead of the expected time of 7pm?? Secondly, the plane was 'boarding' for like 1hour when really 100 people were just standing waiting for them to let them on the plane and.......actually no I won't dampen my first morning in Paris by dwelling on it! I just SO HAPPY to be here - finally in PARIS!!!!

It is so beautiful here! I woke up early to get all pretty before Mia, Parker and I go out for a latte and croissant. Then we are heading straight to the Louvre, and then out for lunch. Hopefully, we can explore some Parisian shops before our dinner/picnic near the Seine river.

I can't wait!

Journal of Sam Duffy

Day 68

Paris is just so so beautiful!

The trains are like less than a pound! A POUND. It's like an arm and a leg in London.

Why is every single meal in Paris always so good? Everything I ate was the best dish I had ever eaten. Everyone is so thin, do they not know how good their food is??

I wasn't able to get to any bars or clubs last night. I always do this when I travel, I can never just relax - I have to try and see everything! And then I pass out by 5pm, like a little old lady that I am.

I miss Paris already! We managed to get breakfast before our flight back, which I was SO grateful for. Thinking of not eating a french meal again makes me tear up. The other thing about Paris, Dr Richards, the people are so attractive and really well dressed!

If you haven't been before (should I call you Sally? I mean its only fair since I don't really know you, but you know so much about me), I shall make you a wee list of things to do in Paris.

Paris

Eat

Basically anywhere BUT I loved:
- LOVE Restaurant
- Macaroons from Ladurée
- Prepare to spend A LOT at one of their chocolate shops!!
- Cute little bakery Boulangerie Utopie
- SAaM

Go See/Do
- Eiffel Tower
- Louvre
- The Wall of Love
- Picnic by the River
- Jewellery Shopping
- Clothes shopping!
- Food market
- Vintage Market

Tips
- Have plenty of money saved up to spend on clothing and jewellery as they will last a lifetime and are so pretty!
- Don't worry about calories (girl, trust me, it ain't the time)
- Travel to Paris by Train (Mia said it was wonderful)

- Don't eat while walking (it's considered rude…apparently, but like a girl might need a snack)
- Go for more than one day
- And don't overdo it on the first day so you can go out to bars and meet cute french boys.

1st February, 2020

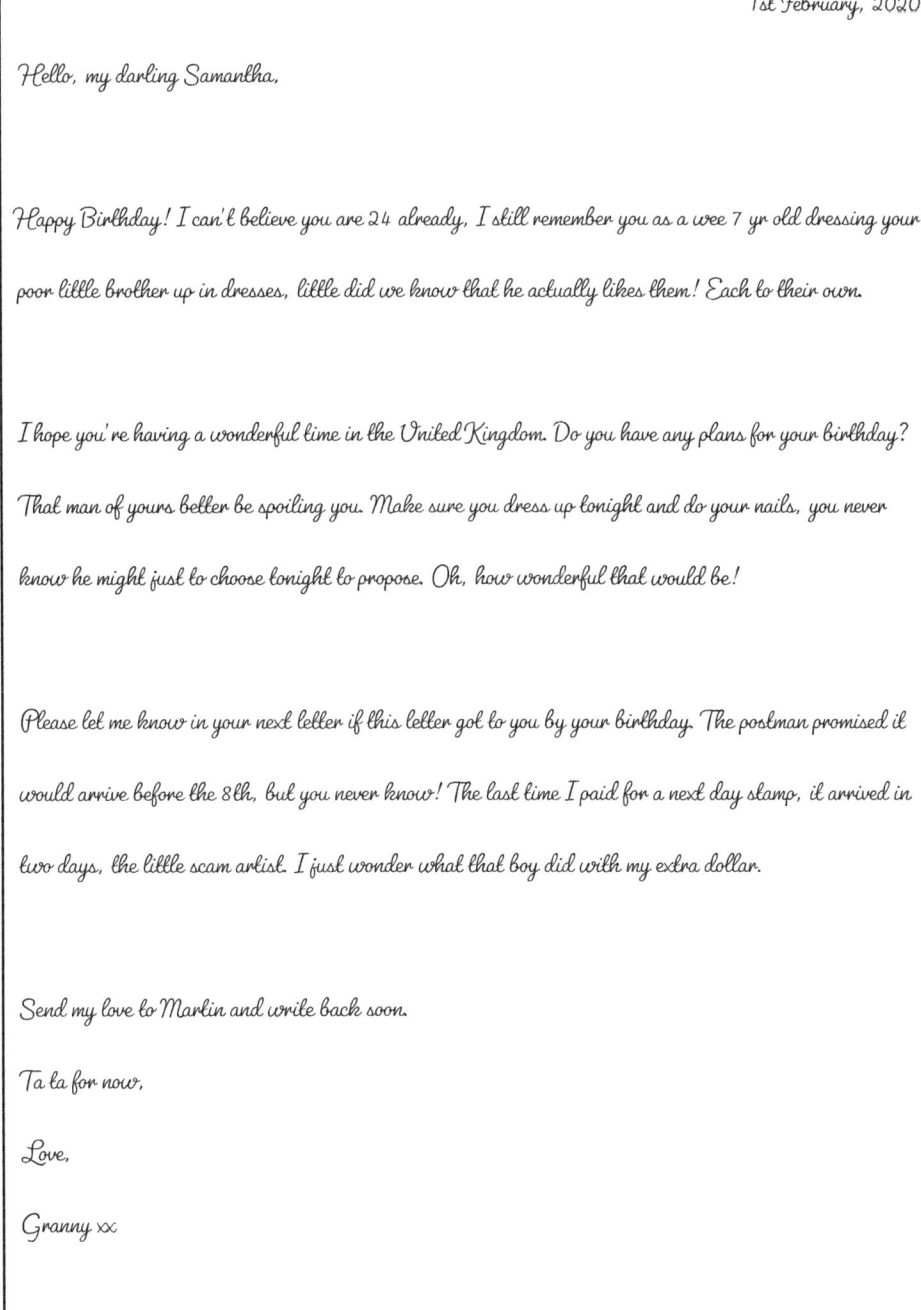

Hello, my darling Samantha,

Happy Birthday! I can't believe you are 24 already, I still remember you as a wee 7 yr old dressing your poor little brother up in dresses, little did we know that he actually likes them! Each to their own.

I hope you're having a wonderful time in the United Kingdom. Do you have any plans for your birthday? That man of yours better be spoiling you. Make sure you dress up tonight and do your nails, you never know he might just to choose tonight to propose. Oh, how wonderful that would be!

Please let me know in your next letter if this letter got to you by your birthday. The postman promised it would arrive before the 8th, but you never know! The last time I paid for a next day stamp, it arrived in two days, the little scam artist. I just wonder what that boy did with my extra dollar.

Send my love to Martin and write back soon.

Ta ta for now,

Love,

Granny xx

To: Sam.Duffy@aol.com

From: Prof.Duffy@aol.com

Subject: Birthday Girl

My little Sammy is a year older, and a year more lovely.
Happy Birthday, darling.

I hope you're having a fun time out with your friends. Your sister told me they were taking you to Paris. Oh, honey, you will love it!

But remember, don't eat too much. I remember the last time you went on holiday you came back looking like a little marshmallow.

I spoke to your grandmother, and she loved your last letter. I was surprised to hear that you didn't tell her about Martin, though at her age I don't know if her heart could take it.

Love you heaps,
Mum xxxoo

Face-to-Face

9:50pm 09/02/20

Lexa Duffy | Online

Call Connecting

Oh my god, how was it? I am so jealous!!
Lexa

                        Um excuse you, aren't you forgetting something?
                        Sam

What?....OH yeah Happy Birthday!!!
Lexa

   Haha, thank you. And Paris was amazing! Everything was so beautiful and the food omg, I still can't comprehend how everything was that delicious?!
                        Sam

You lucky bitch! Did you get Macaroons and eat them by the Eiffel Tower?
Lexa

       I did, but not by the Eiffel Tower. Although, I did have a croissant and coffee by it!
                        Sam

I wish I could have gone with you!
Lexa

                        You could of, if you knew how to save!
                        Sam

Hey I do know how, thank you. I just need a JOB to save.
Lexa

                        Mmm, oh guess what lovely birthday messages I got.
                        Sam

Haha is it one of mum's special messages?
Lexa

Yup, and to top it off, I got a letter from Granny. She wants me to 'send her love to Martin', and to get my nails done just incase now is when he is going to propose. And hmm, for some, weird, unknown reason, I don't know, but I don't think he will be proposing anytime soon? Plus, she sent about 10 NZ stamps inside of it for me. I don't even know if I can use them here …I might look it up.
Sam

Oh god, she didn't?! Poor Granny, you really should write to her more. She is just worried about you, now that you're so far away.
Lexa

I know, I know, I feel bad, but I always forget to write back, and then it's been ages, and I feel weird responding so late. Also, with mum saying it was a 'good thing you didn't tell Granny about it', like the shock of me being pathetically dumped and now single will kill her! I somehow don't have the motivation to write to Granny about how well my life is going right now.
Oh, and that's not all! Mum also managed to throw in a 'now let's not get fat' comment in there too.
Sam

I never know how she manages to put in so many blows into such a nice and short sounding message.
Lexa

Yeah, which makes it way worse. Like you're all 'aww this is sweet…oh wait…oh okay never mind, I'm sad again'.
Sam

Haha I wonder if she knows she is doing it? Anyway, did you get any cool presents??
Lexa

Well... from my boyfriend, I got a really really big shiny engagement ring. But the thing is, it's the same colour as his completion - invisible. So there's that. Ah, a lovely email from mum. Nothing from either of my siblings *cough cough* .
Sam

Oh, you're so dramatic! And it's like you don't know that I can barely afford my student accommodation.
Lexa

I know! I'm just feeding my own self-pity. But I can't help it, it's so hungry! But no, I did get a really really nice gift. So, I thought Mia and Parker were coming with me to Paris as my birthday present, but at like 6pm on Saturday when I was too tired to not be in bed, they knocked on my door with a big box filled with a variety of mini cakes from a french bakery!
Sam

That is so nice of them! You have the best flatmates!
Lexa

I know, too nice, it makes me feel so guilty! But man were they crazy good cakes, especially when you eat them in bed while watching French TV shows.
Sam

You are so lucky...So how was traveling at, like this time?
Lexa

What do you mean?
Sam

You know, the virus that shall not be named.
Lexa

Ahh, yeah I was actually a bit nervous about it ae! Like, I almost thought about not going. Because I read that there are quite a few cases in France

now, and even one or two here in Brighton. But I was cautious about washing my hands and everything. So I should be fine.
Sam

Oh, that's good! It's kinda scary what's happening right now. Remember when you got Swine Flu?
Lexa

Yes and no. I was like 12. But I do remember that I lost 5 kgs in a week!
Sam

Yeah, because you slept for five whole days! You fricken weirdo. If you got it now...
Lexa

I would be a lot thinner.
Sam

...Sam don't joke about this. Like this actually seems serious.
Lexa

I'm sorry! Truely I am. I just don't want to give into my inner fears by actually talking about it. Also, it's super confusing because the PM here says it's just like the regular flue but with a different name - he's still hugging and shaking the hands of everyone he meets.
Sam

Mmmm, just be careful, and wash your hands, and don't touch randoms.
Lexa

Aww, but I LOVE touching randoms! Anyway, I am fucking knackered, good night!
Sam

Night! And happy birthday.
Lexa

To: Sam.Duffy@aol.com
From: anderson@GamingCo.com
Subject: 2020 Game Conferences

Heya Samantha,

Would you be able to send me through a scanned copy of your Passport?

I need to buy tickets and get hotels booked for the game conferences this year before they are all expensive and sold out.

Mark did mention that you were coming with us?
In short, we need someone to help set up stalls, talk to people at the conferences and take photos for our socials. I will book you in as an attendee. Might be beneficial for you to attend some of the talks, to learn more about the industry.

I have attached the 2020 Conference Itinerary.

Sorry I know it's a lot of travel.

- A

Gaming Conferences 2020

Nordic Gaming Conference 2020 (NGC)

Sweden 26th May - 29th May 2020

E3

LA, USA 9th June - 11th June

Games Com

Germany 25th - 29th August

PAX West

Melbourne, Australia 31st August - 2nd September

Journal of Sam Duffy

Day 72

Can this year get any better?!!

My boss just sent me a fucking list of places THEY are sending me to for WORK... I am being paid to travel! Like what the fuck.
I get to go to Germany, Sweden, L.A, and Melbourne for free!

Well.. not for free because I am definitely going to be spending my free afternoons out finding "hot locals in my area" (lol & ew) at the really cool and trendy bar. Omg, what if I end up having like one boy who is deeply, sole crushingly in love with me in each place?? Like a rom-com. And then they all come to Brighton wanting to be with me, and I can't decide who to be with - like in Mamma Mia 2.

This is going to be great!

Also, some of my friends who I haven't seen since Uni are now living in Melbourne, and I could probably go see them!!

I am so fucking glad I took this job and moved to Brighton. Fuck Martin. I can't wait to rub it in his stupid little face. Bitch boy.

Journal of Sam Duffy

Day 81

It has been almost a month of going to the gym 5 times a week! Being single really frees up your time..a lot.
Before I would just sit in my room crying and then eating and then crying again because I was getting fat. But now that I'm filling that time with the gym I definitely don't feel as lonely.

AND I have made so much progress already! I went from being able to do 20 female pushups (which is such a sexist term for that exercise and undermines the strength females are actually capable of so I do <u>not</u> endorse this terminology at all!!), and now, I can do 3 normal pushups! I wanna look like Lara Croft in Tomb Raider.

I almost forgot! Mia and I made gym friends! And they are British - thank god coz I always dreamed that coming to the UK I would have all these dinner parties with my suave British friends. Yet I have only made one friend, who is Australian, which lets face (I'm sorry) is basically a New Zealander. So not much different than my friends back home. I thought I would be more cultured, interesting and like grown moving here...Oh shit I'm rambling, ANYWAY, yes sooo excited to have made some friends at the gym. We have already organised going to the next Friday spin class together! I'm gonna see if I can organise a group brunch next time we hang out! Then us four will be like Sex and the City, but in Brighton, and multi-cultural...and younger.

Journal of Sam Duffy

Day 83

It has been a while since I've talked about Martin and the whole 'break up recovery'. Since creating the New Years resolution to not stalk Martin or his...socials anymore, I have to try not to think about him or the whole situation, or I get fidgety. It's really fucking hard not to have a quick peek and unblock him to see if he has messaged me yet.

And, I know I talk a big game of finding a cute boy and all that. But the truth is I never thought I would have to be finding some else to date. The idea of kissing or having sex with anyone else than Martin scares the shit out of me! Like omg, I can't flirt! I get way into my own head - surely you can understand that about me by now Dr Richards (Sally? You never emailed to say if that was okay). And the small talk, and the not knowing if you should get up early to avoid the awkwardness of a one night stand or if you should stay to give him the chance to show you he wants you to stay. I'm not cool enough for one night stands!
I have no idea how I'm ever going to find someone else.

Break up recovery 30%

Face-to-Face

11:30pm 28/02/20

Lexa Duffy | Online

Call Connecting

Ohhh someone looks good!!
Lexa

> Well, thank you! I have officially lost all 5kgs of my break up weight, and look at my arm muscle.
> Sam

Dammmmn 5kgs! Good for you. You always looked beautiful - what I meant is you look a lot happier, like more glowy, from not angry picking your non-existent pimples, and your eyes are no longer puffy from crying all the time.
Lexa

> Ohhhhh right, right. Thanks for clearing that up...
> Sam

I've been spending like all my time on Pinterest looking at places we should visit when I come up to see you. Can you take two weeks off work instead of one? I thought we could do Paris, and then Rome, Florence, Venice and then go to Greece...
Lexa

> Lexa did you not hear about what's happening in Italy?
> Sam

Yes. I'm not coming up until April which is still like two months away...
Lexa

> More like a month
> Sam

...and it will be fine by then! Plus if it isn't then I will just stay in Brighton with you, and we can go travelling around the UK instead.
Lexa

> Ahhh, okay. Are you sure you still want to come? It kind of seems like it's getting quite serious in Italy, like a lot of people are sick. Countries in Europe have started closing their borders to people coming back from Italy.
> — Sam

Well, the travel agency hasn't contacted me or cancelled my flights, so I'm pretty sure you're overreacting.
Lexa

> Lex, what if you get sick over here? You would have to spend your two weeks holiday, and all of your savings, in a hospital bed in quarantine.
> — Sam

I will be safe, and I'll wash my hands! It will be fine Sam! You've always been so dramatic.
Lexa

> Dramatic? Lex, there's a fucking outbreak...okay, I'm going before I start yelling at you.
> — Sam

Fine.
Lexa

> Fine.
> — Sam

March 2020

Journal of Sam Duffy

Day 91

You would think after 2 months of walking a total of 1 hour and a half to and from work I would be so much fitter and not be sweaty or tired getting to work. But nope. Still sweaty, still exhausted. Still having to get in 5 mins earlier than everyone else just so I can sit on the toilet to recover and wipe off the sweat before anyone sees me.

I'm so tired of walking to work. I wish I could work from home. I would save SO much time just from walking to work. I could sleep in! And if I had like 10mins of waiting for someone to reply or like that awkward 'i've finished all my work today but still have 20mins till 5pm' I could just do chores around the house :(

Journal of Sam Duffy

Day 93

My god. I feel like I'm living in one of those natural disaster movies, but in the intro bit where everyone has been ignoring the signs for ages, and now only realising 'Woah maybe I should be cautious about this very real thing that is happening". But, like as you're watching the movie you're like, 'oh dude you are way too late to only now be cautious now". Yeah, I feel like I'm living in that right now…. how have humans survived this long?

The strangest part! Quite a few people now in the UK are sick - I think about 150 people, and I've already noticed fewer people are turning up to the gym and hogging the machines. But the most grounding realisation of how bad it is, is that guys at the gym are (at least the first I have ever seen of this), spraying and wiping off the sweat from the equipment they have just used. I almost fainted with shock and delight!

Working out to an almost empty gym, with everyone furiously wiping down the equipment and tv screen right in front of you is blaring out the latest horrifying news really takes the intensity out of your work out songs. Like my favourite gym song that always gets me motivated is Kanye's song 'Black Skinhead', and now when I listen to it - all I can think is, 'ahh stop breathing so hard'. It's so dumb, but my mind can't hear it any other way now.

Journal of Sam Duffy

Day 99

Every morning now, I have this weird routine of googling the new daily infection rate for the UK and reporting it to my workmate Jarred, who literally couldn't care less but finds my obsession hilarious. It helps me be lighthearted about it and stuff, but at the same time... how are people at work not talking about this or like concerned?

I've also noticed a lot less people out on the streets walking to work, AND fewer people on the buses...it feels so strange. Like, no one is talking about it, but you can notice the tension in the air. Is this a British thing? I did hear British people didn't like talking about uncomfortable matters.

Anyway, my daily walks to work have gotten WAYYY worse. Like okay, I definitely get everyone's concern and why they try to avoid walking close to me. But it's just because its ice-cold outside and I'm wearing like 5 layers while speed walking. So yeah I'm sweating a lot, a little red maybe and yes, my nose runs from the confusion of hot and cold. But I AM NOT CONTAGIOUS!!

Journal of Sam Duffy

Day 103

I do not feel 100% - maybe 70%.
Last night Mia, Parker and I went out to the pub for a casual 'Friday night drinks'. It was casual at first but it never ever ends with just one pint but with 4 pints, a few drunken cigs and a trip to McDonald's.

I smell nasty. I slept in my clothes and last nights make up. The smell of smoke has covered my clothes and now bedding. My pores reek of alcohol, and it's like stained the air in my room.
I got to clean my sheets, clean my room and open the window for the whole day no matter how cold it is outside…but I'll do it when I feel better. Right now I've got to have a 20min shower, 10 coffees and a huge greasy breakfast.

Last night was so much fun though! We planned a trip to Ireland for St Patrick's day. I am so excited. It's next Tuesday so it should be all good to travel there for two days. I haven't heard any lockdown warnings from the government yet! I am so so excited - I can finally write granny back and tell her about my trip to Ireland! I can't wait, though I do need to book time off for Tuesday and Wednesday.

JetEasy

London → Dublin, Ireland

Total price from
£30

Tues, 17th March 8:00 - 9:00   1hr   0 Stops
EasyJet   LGW-IRE

1 Free Carry On   0 Checked On Bags

Temple Bar Hotel

Standard Double Room
Max persons: 2

1 double bed

1 night, 1 adult

£77
March 17–18

4.3 Stars

Contemporary rooms & suites in a sleek lodging with a sophisticated restaurant & vibrant bar.

Journal of Sam Duffy

Day 104

<u>Dublin Ireland Itinerary</u>

9.30am - Arrive at the hotel

10.00am - Coffee at Love Supreme Cafe

10.30am - Visit Trinity College

12.00pm - Explore Temple Bar area

2.00pm - Late brunch at Thundercut Alley

3.30pm - Shopping at St George's Arcade

6.00pm - Drinks at Temple Bar Pub

To: Sam.Duffy@aol.com

CC: GamingCo Staff

From: Anderson@GamingCo.com

Subject: Work Safety Precautions

Team,

I have been watching the numbers very closely over the past couple of months. I have come to the realisation that the amount of new cases is growing exponentially here in the UK.

Since the government is still not taking action, I bloody well will.

As of today, everyone will be working from home. This is a necessary precaution. I know it will be hard for some of you, but we have to make sure to protect the health of our employees.

Don't come into the office today, if you need a computer to work from or any other office supplies, please let me know, and I will drop them off to you.

Stand-up will be conducted virtually.

I will let everyone know when it is safe for everyone to come back into the office.

Wash your hands, wear a mask and gloves, be safe everyone.

- A

Journal of Sam Duffy

Day 105

Holy shit!!

I can't believe it has finally happened. I was watching the news and new daily cases every day at work for weeks now, wondering when my boss was going to make the call, and now he has!

I officially get to work from home now on in! Woohoo, I'm so fucking excited. I don't have to walk to work, I can sleep in!

It will be weird going back into work next month like I know I will definitely be gutted when we get the all-clear. I wonder if this will give me a chance to prove to my boss I can work from home so I can do this not just for the month but for the rest of the year??!

Though reading the email this morning, I got to admit I was a little taken back. I know I was expecting it but like it didn't hit home the severity of this virus until I read the email…

Ohhh maybe I should cancel our trip to Ireland this week? Will have to check in with M and Parker.

Messages

Group Text from M, Parker

> Hey, I think we need to talk about Ireland.
> I know we have tickets booked to go in just a few days, but work just told everyone to work from home.
> I think this virus is actually getting quite serious.
> Sam
> Read 10.13am

Omg, no way! But we aren't in lockdown yet?!
M
Read 10.14am

My work has been talking about it for a while now too. We'll be working from home by Friday for sure.
Parker
Read 10.14am

> Yeah :/ like if work is worried enough to get everyone to stay home - should we be going to Ireland?
> Sam
> Read 10.15am

I was thinking that.
Parker
Read 10.15am

Nooo, we have to! Parker you only finally just got some time off work, and the government still isn't saying anything about going into a lockdown. I think if we just stay mindful and cautious, we will be fine!
M
Read 10.16am

Parker is Typing

That's right M, but idk what if the UK goes into lockdown while we are in Ireland. We could be stuck there.

Sam
Read 10.18am

It sucks but it's too risky.

Parker
Read 10.18am

The tickets are refundable, so we can always go in April or May x

Sam
Read 10.19am

Yeah okay :(I was just really looking forward to it.

M
Read 10.22am

I'll make it up to you babe, promise x

Parker
Read 10.22am

You better ;) xx

M
Read 10.23am

Ew guys! Keep it out of group chat, please.

Sam
Read 10.23am

Journal of Sam Duffy

Day 107

This is the strangest thing.

Today is St Patrick's day, so of course, you assume a day of drinking, going to parties, maybe doing a pub crawl or street party. But oh, no! Last night the government sent out a notice saying no pubs could be open for St Patricks and if you were seen outside with alcohol then you will be fined! Really seems like the government might be starting to put virus safety restrictions in.

Anyway, Parker, Mia and I decided that we weren't going to stay at home, being sad, watching Love Island, thinking about how we could be in Ireland right now. Instead we decided to go out for a drink. Okay, yeah so no pubs can be open, but they still serve alcohol at restaurants! So, we got dinner at this Japanese place down the street, sat outside and had a few wines with our sushi. But omg it was so strange! Like 'what the hell has happened' type of strange.

Today is St Patrick's! ST PATRICKS! People are meant to be out and roaming the streets being all drunk and happy, but there was no one out. There were probably only a few people in the restaurant, but the street was bare of foot traffic! I saw one group of friends dressed up in green drunkenly walking home. Though it just looked a bit sad tbh.

I don't think it has really hit me the gravity of this. It's like watching a zombie movie but being in it, just watching on the sidelines with a big bucket of popcorn.

Messages

Today 9am

GOV.UK CORONAVIRUS ALERT

New rules are now in force: you must stay home. More information and exemptions at **gov.uk/coronavirus** or text COVID19.

Stay at home, protect lives.

COVID19

GOV.UK CORONAVIRUS ALERT

New rules and guidelines are now in force.

You must stay at home. Exemptions include one hour walk a day and trips to the supermarket. For more information and exemptions at **gov.uk/coronavirus**.

Stay at home, protect lives.

Messages

Group Text from M, Parker

> Did you guys get a text about lockdown??
> Sam
> Read 9.45am

Yes! So crazy!
M
Read 9.45am

About time too.
Parker
Read 9.46am

> Wait, does this mean I can't get coffee?
> Sam
> Read 10.46am

Nah girl! We're still open and everything, but we can't allow anyone to come inside the cafe. Serving takeaway coffee only now.
M
Read 9.47am

> Oh thank god!
> Sam
> Read 9.47am

We should probably get supplies.
M
Read 9.50am

Ohh emergency snacks!
M
Read 9.51am

Haha. I meant more toilet paper, canned foods, shit like that.
M
Read 9.51am

Ew canned food! Sounds way to dramatic, I mean we're not gonna run out of canned food anytime soon. But those damn hoarders might stock up on all the good chips before we get to them!
M
Read 9.52am

> Haha, Parkers right though M, I tried going to the supermarket on my way home last week and a 4 pack of toilet paper cost me £5!
> Sam
> Read 9.53am

Yeah. Things are nuts. We should prepare just in case. Though we can also stock up on snacks as well xx
M
Read 9.54am

Woohoo!!
M
Read 9.54am

To: Sam.Duffy@aol.com

From: Prof.Duffy@aol.com

Subject: Lockdown

Darling,

I heard about the United Kingdom going into lockdown. I hope you're doing okay.

Apparently, New Zealand is about to go into lockdown ourselves. The prime minister is calling all kiwis living aboard to come home now before they shut off the borders. But honestly darling, I don't think you should fuss. You have a great job and friends over there now, and if you come back now all you'll be doing is sleeping in your old high school bedroom.

This will all blow over soon. Chin up, and make sure you use that full hour of daily exercise.

Love,
Mum xoxo

To: Sam.Duffy@aol.com

From: Richards.Sally@London.ac.uk

Subject: Recap on First Session

Hi Samantha,

Concerning current events, I just wanted to email and remind you that you are still expected to keep on top of your daily diary entries.

The new government guidelines and current news coverage of world events will be very stressful and detrimental to most people at this time. I have included a list of ways to reduce stress and improve your mental health during this tough time.

- One minute breathing exercise: 4 second breath in, 4 second breath out.
- Meditate 5 - 10 minutes a day.
- Yoga for 15 minutes a day increases blood flow, and improves mood.
- Set and keep to a regular schedule.
- Exercise 30 minutes a day.
- Get plenty of rest - 7 to 9 hours of sleep each night.
- Drink lots of water and green tea.
- Find a hobby you enjoy, such as Painting or reading.
- Avoid alcohol and drugs.

Stay safe.

Kind Regards,
Dr Sally Richards.

Journal of Sam Duffy

Day 109

Working from home is the fucking best!!

I get to sleep in until 8.50am. I "don't have a webcam" so no one can see me during stand up or meetings which means 1. I get to wake up like a boy, where I wake up 10 mins before work, shower, have coffee, and I'm ready. 2. I don't have to wear makeup. 3. I don't have to find a new outfit to wear every day. 4. I don't have to wear pants!

As I am writing this, I am in my undies, wearing an oversized t-shirt - with no bra! I feel so free. This is me, living my best life!

Though my 'break up glow up' goal has really started to go downhill. I have not left the house, I can't go to the gym anymore, and I have almost eaten a months supply of chips and chocolate within less than a week :/

Also, I really need to find a new place to work from. Right now I'm using my bedroom floor as I'm using a work desktop computer so I need a desk, but I can't fit a desk in my room. But omg my bum is so damn numb, and my back is killing me!

...I could use the kitchen maybe...I'll keep you updated Dr Richards.

Journal of Sam Duffy

Day 110

New office local has been found, measured, tested and verified!

Mia very generously helped me in my endeavour and confirmed that this bedroom floor was indeed not acceptable for a badass business bitch. Still, neither was the noisy and distracting scene of our shared kitchen. I know what you're thinking, 'but where will you place your desk if not the kitchen or bedroom?', and well I say this - hallways.

Okay okay so I know it sounds lame, but we have a big like hallway area just before the stairs, but since no one will be going outside anyway, the space is just unused and very quiet. I could even fit a small desk and chair in there. Oh and the best bit is it has this large old window that I can sit next to and just people watch/spy on our next-door neighbours when I get bored at work.

Mia's going to help me assemble the desk I brought online. This is so exciting!

Journal of Sam Duffy

Day 112

You would be ashamed of me, Dr Richards. I have not exercised in a week. The type of exercise I do now is the odd trip to the supermarket for supplies or to get coffee, and that totals about 15 mins tops of literally just standing.

But I just feel like it's so much unnecessary effort now. Like I have to shower, brush my hair, put on jeans and makeup just to go outside for less than an hour??

I mean I know makeup isn't important and I should feel comfortable as I am and all of that shit. But the fact is - I don't. I just don't feel confident without makeup or wearing 'acceptable clothing'. I know that's really fucked up and I should work on that...Idk I just get so self-conscious without having some sort of barrier between me and the outside world - yah know?

Though this would be the best time to build up my no-makeup confidence. Literally, no one is outside! It's like a ghost town. Every day I would hear people from the street below talking or arguing or laughing, and now it's just quiet and spooky.

Anyway yes it's a ghost town, but there's a little part of me that taunts me with thoughts like 'but as soon as you don't wear make up is when you run into a bunch of hot men', you know shit like that.

I have so much free time now, I'm struggling with my rule not to stalk Martin. I just want to have a wee peek! A wee sneaky, small peek :(

To stop this insatiable and detrimental habit from taking over my life, I have ordered books to read. SO many books that I spent £100! £100 on books!! But it will mean that I will have one book to read a week and no time for thoughts of Martin being stuck at home, alone with his hot new British girlfriend.

Journal of Sam Duffy

Day 113

Mia and Parker have been fighting quite a bit lately. I hate it. I can hear their yelling matches through the walls, and it makes me so sad. They are such a cute couple and were so happy, I hate that now because of lockdown they've become angry with each other.

Stupid pandemic.

Oh, sorry Dr Richards (...Sally?), how rude to mention the fighting and not delve into the goss. And yes, I hate that they are fighting, but I also do thoroughly enjoy some gossip!

Okay so, Parker's manager decided to quit just before lockdown, so while everyone at his office is working from home, Parker has to go into an empty office at 7am and do his work plus his old manager's job. Which is awful, sometimes he doesn't come home until twelve. Obviously, Mia isn't happy about this and wishes that he just quits work. But that makes Parker angry apparently because they need the money and can't afford to be unemployed right now.

I can see it from both their perspectives. Like Mia just misses him, and Parker is just trying his hardest to provide for them. In some way, I feel like it's worse not having someone clearly in the wrong. If someone was wrong, at least you could figure out what could be said or done to fix things. In this situation, you can't really do anything than just letting it be fucking shit and run its course.

I really REALLY hope they don't break up. Being part of the online 'Brighton Girls Group' I've heard a lot of people have been breaking up during lockdown. I don't want that to happen to Mia and Parker :(

Journal of Sam Duffy

Day 114

HOLY SHIT! I knew my new office space was going to be great! This morning I started work, sipping on my cup of instant coffee when something caught the corner of my eye. I turned to see that my next-door neighbour from the building across from me, had entered his kitchen shirtless! I almost spat out my coffee!

How did I not know I had a hot neighbour???

Well, I couldn't see much of him since he's so far away, but I damn well know enough. Amazing body, like washboard abs - maybe he's a surfer?? He's definitely tall, dark brown hair. Can't really make out his facial features but he is cute!

The awkward bit is I was sitting there, right next to the window, mouth gaping open staring at the poor guy, when he turns around and sees me. He was obviously surprised and a bit startled - can't blame him. I did the whole 'oh hi' nod and look back at the computer like I had suddenly received a very important email. ARGGHHH! By the time I looked back over - the hot mystery window man was gone :(

Oh no, I think I need to start wearing pants, and maybe a clean t-shirt.

Journal of Sam Duffy

Day 115

It is day 7 of lockdown, and there seems to be no signs of life. No human or creature roams these empty streets. Nothing stirs the still echoing silence that fills The Lanes.

But seriously, no one is outside right now! I say this a lot, but it's like I'm living in a world where I'm the only survivor, but less fun because I don't get to live in a grocery store or take what I want from abandoned shops.

I went out to get a coffee at my local cafe, the one where Mia works, and it was closed! But I swear I saw M leave for work this morning?

Panic ran through me. Every cafe in the few blocks around me are all closed!! I know there MUST be one coffee shop somewhere in this city that is open - I just gotta find it. Might hunt one down tomorrow.

That decides it though - I will no longer wear makeup or care about my appearance when I leave the apartment. There just simply isn't anyone out to feel self-conscious around anymore!

Messages

Text to M

                                                        Oh my god M, are you okay?
                                                                                                   Sam
                                                                                               Read 1.45pm

Hey girl! Yeah haha, what's up?
M
Read 1.45pm

                                                                        It's just…the cafe's closed?
                                                                                                   Sam
                                                                                              Read 1.46pm

Oh yeah! Sorry girl, I forgot to mention. My boss has decided to only keep one of the cafe's open, so she's moved me to the cafe on the hill.
M
Read 1.47pm

                    :(Wait that isn't the hilltop cafe that's like 20 mins away is it?
                                                                                                     Sam
                                                                                              Read 1.47pm

…maybe x
M
Read 1.47pm

                                                                                Curse my lazy legs :(
                                                                                                 Sam
                                                                                              Read 1.48pm

Haha, I think I heard one cafe is open out near the beachfront. It's quite hidden though.
M
Read 1.49pm

OMG yes thank you! That's the best news I've heard all day. Oh, reminds me, p.s we have a hot new neighbour.

Sam
Read 1.50pm

Nooo! Details please…oh wait, tell me when I get home, I gotta go back to work, Cassandra's giving me the side-eye again xx

M
Read 1.50pm

Face-to-Face

11:30pm 25/03/20

Lexa Duffy | Online

Call Connecting

Heyyy loser

Sam

Why hello. I see you have been embracing the quarantine life?
Lexa

Oh, you have no idea! I was made for this shit. Except why do you look so...fresh and...is that makeup?

Sam

Get out of it!
Lexa

Lex, have you been breaking the rules to go see a boy?

Sam

No, I have not, because technically he is inside my bubble!
Lexa

Your bubble? What the hell does that mean?

Sam

You know, like in your bubble of people who live with you - the only people you're allowed to go to the supermarket with and go on walks with.
Lexa

Lex, he is not in your bubble! You've been dating this guy for like a month, he lives in a flat with lots of other people. You're definitely breaking the rules! For a bloody hookup.
Sam

Hey! It's not just a hookup, I really like him, and I'm like always at his place anyway, so he should count as my bubble. I mean, I haven't been to my flat in five days.
Lexa

Woah, I didn't realise you two were that serious! Does this mean I get to stalk him on social media now?
Sam

Ew no, you can definitely not!... what about you anyway? Any hot new boys lately?
Lexa

What have I taken up a new romance while being in quarantine? Hmm, no, I have not. Which is so weird because you'd think you'd come by a man so easily in lockdown.
The only men in my life right now come from books and tv shows.
Sam

Haha okay whatever! I just know a few of my friends are meeting guys online, and then doing like virtual dates. It sounds cool!
Lexa

Omg, it sounds so awkward and awful! Hell no!
Are you still planning on coming up to the UK?
Sam

Hmmm yeah, I don't know ae. The flights still aren't cancelled and I still really want to go, but I'm not sure if I should come up if everything is going to be closed anyway.

Lexa

> Yeah I hope everything opens back up again by mid-April so I can see you and show you around - but it's probably the wisest decision to not plan on that happening.
>
> Sam

I would be so sad if I couldn't come to see you though! If I can't, then I will definitely come up for Christmas, and maybe we could visit New York for New Years!

Lexa

> Oh, yes, please! That would be amazing, and we could see the ball drop and everything!
>
> Sam

Yes!!

Hey sorry, I got to go, he's making me dinner hehe.

Lexa

Journal of Sam Duffy

Day 116

Mission: Sacred bean juice!

The journey was challenging and treacherous, but oh the glory that awaited me at the end!!

To start off my sacred mission to find a coffee shop, I realised god fucking damn do I love living in a beachfront city where the streets are almost empty, and you don't know anyone:

1. I no longer get social anxiety because there is no around to overwhelm my delicate ~~little~~ big brain.
2. If there is someone around you can avoid them like the plague because...well you know.
3. You aren't going to stumble into anyone you know, so you can wear leggings, stained over-sized jumpers, no-makeup, and you don't have to even brush your hair! Just put that thang in a bun, and you're done (though I still wear deodorant because it would be rude not to).

It's the best thing ever. I thought it would be hard, but it's like revolutionary! I feel no fucking shred of shame, and I don't get ANY judgemental looks because the only people I see - are doing the exact same thing!

I was never a 'go on a walk to make myself feel better' type of person, I have always been 'have ice-cream to feel better' type of gal. Though lockdown is REALLY making me appreciate how nice it is to go outside and go on a walk - Who would have thought?!

Anywayyyy - The mission at hand!
When Mia said it was hard to find, omg she was not wrong! It took me 15 mins of roaming The Lanes near the beach to find it! Though I have to admit I love the location. It's hidden in this tiny alleyway which is filled with flowers and overgrown plants. It's beautiful, AND it's a street away from the beach, so I can order my coffee and get in a thirty-minute walk by the seafront!

Though when I went to order my coffee, there was a really trendy, kinda alty girl severing. I could feel my cheeks burning, and without any foundation, I 100% know I looked like a tomato! She just looked so cool with thick eyeliner, blue hair and a whole bunch of tattoos. While I was standing there in sweatpants and messy hair. And the girl is like the same age as me! Even the guy making coffees looked all cool and tattooed! My god. When I ordered my Mocha, she was like, "what?", so I repeated it, and she still couldn't understand me. I tried explaining it "Like a latte but with chocolate added in", and she was like "Oh! You mean a MOCHA" and looked back at me like the interaction was exhausting. I know I have an accent but DAMN!
If the guy out back didn't make such beautiful coffee...and wasn't so cute, I would definitely not go back.

Though the barista did look familiar, though I can't place where I've seen him before. I noticed he kept looking back at me. Maybe I do know him from somewhere?
Nah he's probably staring at the pure state of me.

Their poor, poor eyes.

Journal of Sam Duffy

Day 118

I went out for another coffee and walk by the beach today! The coffee is so good, and I should really be making sure to look after my mental health and get out of the house at least once a day!

Though while enjoying my coffee, it went down the wrong way and I started choking a little bit which was awful. Usually, if you see someone coughing their lungs out, people would look worried and ask if you're okay. But not anymore! People looked at me in pure disgust and openly changed their direction! I want to yell out 'I'm not sick I'm just choking!' but obviously I couldn't because I was almost dying on my own spit! The worst bit was I was trying my hardest not to cough from pure embarrassment which made me tear up. Long story short - on my walk back to the flat everyone looked at me like I had been crying.

My god what a fucking morning.

Journal of Sam Duffy

Day 119

It's Saturday, and I have not moved from my bed for the past 24 hours unless I have to pee or get snacks.
I have not showered in two days.

Who have I become? Who have I let myself become?

This morning I walked passed the mirror, and the sight of my own reflection made me jump!!! My own face scared me.

My god Dr Richards if only you could see me now!

I gotta get my shit together. From tomorrow morning, I will stick to a schedule, be a proper adult again and look after myself.

Healthy Morning Schedule

6.00am - Wake up and shower

6.30am - Meditate

6.40am - Yoga

7.00am - Breakfast (without watching the News or tv!)

7.30am - Get coffee and go for a walk by the beach

8.00am - Read

9.00am - Work

To-Do Every Day

- Meditate for 5-10 mins
- Yoga
- Get at least a 30min walk
- Read for an hour minimum
- Do not watch the News! (That shit is always making you sad and stressed).
- Eat a damn salad.
- Shower
- Brush hair
- Put on fresh, clean clothes
- Tidy up room

Journal of Sam Duffy

Day 121

I am finally getting my shit back together! I had a wee set back when lockdown first happened, but now I'm back - I've even wore pants while working today!

And I am so glad that I brushed my hair and put on an outfit that wasn't a jumper and sweatpants because guess who served me coffee today?
The cute barista! Oh boy is he cute, that smile! I almost forgot my order. Though I think the girl who usually serves must have asked him to swap when she saw me coming. I don't know why she wouldn't like me that much that she didn't want to take my order! I've only talked to her once :(
Oh no, what if she can't stand to look at me in this state? Maybe it depresses her having to look at me?... Should I start wearing makeup again??

Actually no, I should be happy and confident in my own skin. A really cool cafe girl can't make me feel bad about that!

Journal of Sam Duffy

Day 122

I am going to go bankrupt!
The lockdown is eating up all of my money!
I thought - 'Oh I'll save so much from not buying drinks or going out on the weekends' - but I'm still spending so much money. For example, instead of getting lunch out, I get it delivered, so there's that extra sneaky delivery fee. My supermarket shop is WAY more expensive as I'm eating just all of the snacks, and if you think my wine consumption has gone down in lockdown then you're out of your mind!

Plus I have nothing to do in my free time anymore. I've watched everything good off Netflix. Let's be honest, they aren't popping out shows like they use to (which is actually very fair as movie production would be on halt with the rest of the world). Sorry, I'm rambling again - okay so, the books I spent £100 on and thought would last me a month. Well nope, two weeks is all it took to read four books! I just ordered 6 more to hopefully tie me over for April. This level of book consumption is not healthy for my bank account.

p.s I brought 3 modern romance novels. The website I ordered it from called it a Chick flick. Which is such a sexist term. Why is there no

Broflicks? Because for some reason, what females find entertaining or exciting is deemed to be silly.

Anyway, I also ordered 3 mystery books - so I don't overdo it on the whole unobtainable romanticisms and create unhealthy romantic ideals/expectations (which I will most definitely do).

p.p.s. Agatha Christie can fucking write a damn mystery novel. I mean, I knew she was a famous author and everything, but only my grandparents talked about her work. I am so glad she wrote so many novels because I'm hooked. It's like when I stumbled upon a tv show and am like 'eh I'll give it a go', and I absolutely love it, and then realise it also has a healthy 10 seasons.

April 2020

Messages
Text to M

                                I saw mystery window boy again today!
                                                                Sam
                                                               Read 5.43pm

Ohh that's like what 5 days in a row now?!
M
Read 5.43pm

                       Every morning at 9 am he's there sitting by the table reading.
                                                                     Sam
                                                               Read 5.44pm

OMG, he is so sitting there to get a few glimpses at yah!
M
Read 5.45pm

     Idk though - he always leaves at like 11am. Maybe he is just sitting there to read plus when he happens to glance over he does this awkward acknowledging smile - like 'hey, yes, we are both in each others line of sight'.
                                                                         Sam
                                                                      Read 5.46pm

No way!! You're overthinking all of this.
M
Read 5.46pm

                                      Am I because the latter sounds nuts.
                                                                        Sam
                                                                         Read 5.47pm

Girl, this a pandemic people have got find new ways to flirt and apparently that dude is trying to window flirt with you.
M
Read 5.48pm

haha still…
Sam
Read 5.49pm

Okay look, I have never seen him reading there before, and I've lived here six months longer than you. And what weirdo chooses to read from an uncomfortable dining room chair, knowing there's a hot girl across the street staring, especially when there is a comfy couch and bed to read from?? Yeah, no one, because that boy is trying to flirt!
M
Read 5.50pm

Hahaha yeah okay, maybe you're right!
Sam
Read 5.50pm

Damn straight! See I told you, you looked babe'n even without makeup
M
Read 5.51pm

Thanks M xx
Idk why, I just feel like unkept not wearing it, plus he can't see me clearly. All I can make out of him is like far distance details.
Sam
Read 5.53pm

Do I need to come over there and slap you?
M
Read 5.54pm

♡
Sam
Read 5.54pm

Journal of Sam Duffy

Day 125

I woke up this morning to the sounds of doors slamming and Parker and Mia yelling at each other. It was 6.30am! On a Saturday! Apparently, Parker's boss wants him to work this weekend and head into the office this morning.

Parker's been working A LOT recently. Usually, he would work long hours from Monday to Friday. Now I can't even remember when he had a day off or when the last time I saw him was...February? No no, it was definitely some time in March.

His work is going to burn him out. I hope they ease up on him soon.

... I think I heard him leave. I'm going back to bed.

Journal of Sam Duffy

Day 127

Progress with window boy has been made!
How is M always right about this stuff??
He is always at the window reading at 9am every day of the week, no matter what. We have gone from the shy glances and awkward smiles to lingering side-eyed glances and warm, welcoming smiles. My stomach is a rack of nerves, just thinking about it. I'm actually excited to get up in the morning now! Like I now have an actual reason to shower and dress.

I feel fucking ridiculous getting excited about this. I don't even really know what he actually looks like and I haven't even spoken a word to him. I could literally be just some crazy girl next door to him.

...and yet I can't help but get a little bit excited and daydream about it.

It's like a damn rom-com, and I'm Meg Ryan!
The only problem is - I have no idea how to get his number or confirm in some way that he is trying to flirt with me...

Face-to-Face

11:08pm 09/04/20

Lexa Duffy | Online

Call Connecting

My flight got cancelled.
Lexa

> Well hello to you too...wait what?
> Sam

I got an email this morning from my travel agent that the airline cancelled the flight to London.
Lexa

> Aw fuck! But I was so looking forward to seeing you and showing you around - hey wait wasn't your flight meant to be in a few days? Can they cancel it that close?
> Sam

Apparently, they can. I don't know we did kind of expect it though. And I got travel insurance, so I'll get refunded.
Lexa

> Argh, well hopefully I will be able to see you in December!
> Sam

Yeah definitely, everything should be fine by then! It might just mean we'll have even more money to spend while I'm up!
Lexa

> Ohh good point! I love spending money just sucks I never have much of it. Hey did you see that TiKToK I sent you?
> Sam

Haha yes, I almost cried! The content on that site is really improving recently.
Lexa

Yeah, it's like the only thing doing well through lockdown. Have you been on Instagram? My whole feed is dead, no one is posting anything.
Sam

Yeah! No one has anything to post anymore, and if they do, it makes people pissed off. Like, I unfollowed someone yesterday because she kept posting about her indoor gym and pool and tennis court, but with captions like 'Argh quarantine' and 'I'm so bored'.
Lexa

Oh ew! Fair enough. How's, the boyfriend?
Sam

Ah..um he's good.
Lexa

Why are you whispering and being weird? Omg, are you still at his place?
Sam

...No.
Lexa

Holy crap this must be serious! Have you guys said 'I love you's' yet? Have you seen his parents?
Sam

Omg Sam! We've only been dating for like five months now.
Lexa

So that doesn't matter, not when it comes to loveeee. Wait you didn't answer my question, were you avoiding it because you do lovvvee him.
Sam

Ew, Sam get out of it!
Lexa

I can't wait to see your new lover boy! Is he there, can I talk to him?
Sam

Call Ended

Journal of Sam Duffy

Day 132

The cute barista now calls me 'Mocha girl'! I don't know if I've just been reading way too many romance novels recently, but it seems like he lights up when he sees me coming. It's dumb, I know, and I'm overthinking it. Plus I'm pretty sure baristas flirt with customers all the time that's how they get bigger tips...even though you don't tip in the UK.

But today it was just him working today, I asked him what happened to the angry girl, and he laughed. We actually talked for a bit, until I got way too anxious once I realised I was actually having a great conversation with an attractive person. For some reason, just the thought of it potentially leading to some sort of romance for me my brain is like 'ah nope'. As soon as my payment cleared, I darted off to the side of the wall, which ended the whole conversation. The worst bit is I could tell he was surprised and wanted to keep talking.

What the fuck is my problem!!

p.s I did I mention he has an Irish accent??

Journal of Sam Duffy

Day 133

Easter Sunday....what can I say? Have I saved my whole hoard of chocolate to be eaten only during this weekend? No. Have I been eating chocolate bunnies every day for the past two weeks? Yes. Have I gained weight? Oh, most definitely. Will I pretend like I haven't and act like eating one egg is way too much chocolate and then go back into my room and eat more? Yes.

I love Easter!

Today is the only day of the year, I can openly eat a mound of chocolate, and it is socially acceptable. Since we can't go out to a park and have an easter picnic, Parker, Mia and I were going to have a picnic up on the rooftop...except it rained. So instead we had a flat easter picnic on our lounge floor but with some....*cough* green tea. If you get my drift.

It was so much.
Though I don't want you to get the wrong impression, Dr Richards. I never do it, just occasionally, on special occasions. I will say I feel so much better now, like more relaxed :)

Messages

Today 9.00am

GOV.UK CORONAVIRUS ALERT

Current guidelines and rules have been extended until 17/05/2020. Rules as still in place: you must stay home. More information and exemptions at **gov.uk/coronavirus** or text COVID19.

Stay at home, protect lives.

Journal of Sam Duffy

Day 138

Lockdown has been extended for another month. Is it awful if I'm slightly relieved/glad? It is, isn't it??

Hear me out, I definitely wish this virus would fuck right off and there are aspects of this whole thing that is really scary. I watch the news more than I have ever done, and every day there is something new that makes me want to cry and curl up into a ball. And I want my old flatmates back! The ones that would have Friday drinks with me, play board games with after work when we're bored and who made me smile when I could hear them in the lounge laughing at each other. Not the ones who wake me up every other morning fighting and yelling :(

But then my god damn laziness gets the better of me. Things would be 200% better if everything went back to normal, but then, I think of walking to work and being sweaty, nose dripping and looked at, and having to say goodbye to empty streets and hello to social anxiety.

I feel like this is something I secretly wish for now, and the universe is going to punish me with later on.
Omg, is this the thing old generations have prepared us for? Saying shit like "Be careful with what you wish for", and showing us movies of

people making wishes to a Genie and each wish is granted but altered slightly to be fucking horrible???

...anyway definitely looking forward to another few weeks of not having to walk to work and sleeping in hehe

Messages

Lexa: New Zealand is coming out of lockdown in two weeks!!

Sam: No way! Ours have been extended for another month - which means one more month of being a lazy piece of shit woohoo.

Lexa: Omg you freak!

Lexa: Hey, have you written granny back yet?

Sam: I was going to! I was meant to do it after my trip to Ireland, so I could include some photos of me over there but since that never happened...

Lexa: Oh, right, fair! You can still write though

Sam: And say what? "Hey granny, I hope you're happy to know your little Sammy has been dumped, with no romantic prospects and is living like a homeless person in her own flat"??

Lexa: Argh, you're so dramatic!

Sam: That's what you said last time about the virus and you coming up here and guess who was right and actually very sensible?

Lexa: Ew whatever - just write her back, I'm sure just saying anything will make her happy. She just worries about you.

Sam: Why don't you write to her?

Lexa: Um because I live in the same city as her, not 35 hours away...

Sam: :(

Sam: Okayyyy

Journal of Sam Duffy

Day 140

Mia and Parker were fighting again this morning...
I think it's getting worse. Not only does Mia never get to see him anymore but when she does, Parker just looks wrecked. Like I briefly saw him the other day coming out of the shower and omg, that guy is so stressed out and overworked I barely recognised him. So Mia is not only sad and lonely, she now is really worried about him. Poor Parker.

But since that man has barely any energy and is stressed to the max, anything Mia brings up or says he just snaps at. Like he doesn't have the energy or room to listen. Which only makes them fight more and much louder.

Messages

Text from Parker

Hey Sam, sorry if we woke you this morning. Things have just been crazy.

Parker
Read 9.45am

> Hey, that's all good! I understand things must be tough.
>
> Parker
> Read 9.45am

Yeah. I was hoping you might be able to hang out with Mia today if you're free? She's a bit lonely at the moment, and I want to help cheer her up, but I can't take any time off work.

Parker
Read 9.46am

> That's so sweet! Of course - anything for M :)
>
> Parker
> Read 9.47am

Thanks, Sam.

Parker
Read 9.46am

Journal of Sam Duffy

Day 140

Taking a Duvet day off work to help cheer up Mia was the best fucking idea! And work was so cool about it - they asked no questions, they just said 'have fun, you deserve it.' ♡

And you know what Dr Richards I do deserve - we all deserve a damn duvet day!

...where was I? Oh right cheering up Mia! Sorry, I'm just a wee bit tipsy. We were gonna get ingredients to bake and bitch like we do on Sundays, but then we were like - why not drunken bake?? So we brought orange juice and champagne and made mimosas (how weird is it that as soon as we put orange juice with alcohol, and it suddenly becomes acceptable to get drunk at 10 am?).

We didn't even end up making cookies. We made the dough though! Cookie dough + Mimosa + Bridget Jones diary's is such a great combo. I think we both really needed this. To bitch about EVERYTHING and just get it off our chest yah know?? I feel so much lighter!

M is so amazing she needs to get her mind off everything....she would be such a great like YouTuber or something. One she is outgoing, two super bubbly personality, she's so charismatic - everyone loves M, and she's gorgeous! 1 million followers min - I would give a week tops!

And M is SO right I do need closure! I still have so many unanswered questions. Like how long was he seeing her for? Why did he want her? What happened to us? Do you still love me or think about me or even care what you did to me? I need another drink.

Messages

Text to Don't Answer

> You're a small pussy dick head!
>
> Sent

> I hope you're having a real great time stuck inside with her. How long have you guys been seeing each other huh? There's quite a few questions you've left unanswered coz you couldn't face me like a man!
>
> Sent

> Little pussy ass bitch!
>
> Sent

> I'm Meg Ryan bitch
>
> Sent

> WALTER
>
> Sent

Messages

Text to Unknown Number

Heyyyy so I know you probably don't know me but I'm the girl Martin aka WALTER cheated on to be with you. And I just wanted to know how long have you two been seeing each other and also what makes you so great???

Sent

Journal of Sam Duffy

Day 141

Holy fuck how much did we drink yesterday?
I don't even remember the afternoon. Hopefully, M is okay - I couldn't hear them fighting this morning so she must be out cold.
I did have so much fun, though! I didn't realise how much I need to just vent and relax and take a girls day. I thought I was handling everything fine, but I think I must have just been pushing everything to the back of my mind, so I didn't have to deal with it properly. But somehow that tends to make it worse...

My mouth is so dry I need water but fuck my head is pounding, I don't know how I will be able to walk from my bed to the kitchen. Hopefully, my phone is charging in there because I can't find it.

….So good news I have drunk a gallon of water, had the strongest coffee paired with Paracetamol and plain toast. And I found my phone in the oven. Bad news I found my fucking phone!!
OMG OMG OMG what the FUCK did I do!! AHHHHHHH why did M not stop me! I'm so embarrassed. And all the messages have been 'seen'.
Fuck! Martin must be so happy he left me right now. The worst part is I even texted his new GF (don't ask me how I got it).

....that's what they must be wondering. Fuck they must know I've been stalking her!

My headache has gotten WAY worse

Journal of Sam Duffy

Day 143

Ever since the drunken text incident, I've upped my daily walk from 30mins to the whole 60mins. I just need to get out of the house and clear my mind and avoid the world for a little bit.

As much as I love walks by the beach, it also makes me so sad! Do you know how many dogs I see walking by the beach with their friendly, happy little faces, and can I touch them? No.
Today was significantly worse. The cutest, sweetest little ChowChow (you know, those medium-sized dogs who look so damn cuddly) came up to me all energetic and jumped up on my legs!
The cuteness was too god damn much. I just wanted to pat him! But I could see his owner giving me the stink eye, calling him away. So I looked into his big beautiful eyes and told him to go.

I couldn't stop thinking about it the whole way home...he just wanted a wee pat.

Oh, before I forget - I saw a girl out today wearing makeup, with jeans on and had brushed her hair! It was like seeing an alien!

Face-to-Face

11:30pm 25/04/20

Lexa Duffy | Online

Call Connecting

Hey!
Sam

Hey, haven't seen your stupid face in a while. What's up?
Lexa

Nothing much. Just workin'. Oh, I saw a girl all dressed up in The Lanes the other day.
Sam

Whoa! What a rare and odd sighting!
Lexa

I know, right!
Sam

What do you think the story is behind that?
Lexa

Mmm, I don't know. Maybe she walks past a hottie each day and is trying to get their attention?
Sam

Haha oh for sure! Is it sad that this type of shit is now really entertaining for us?
Lexa

Definitely very, very sad. So what's new with you?
Sam

Nothing. Just the usual. supermarket, walk, home....
Lexa

Cool...
Sam

………
Lexa

………
Sam

An hour later

Hey, I'm gonna go.
Sam

Aw okay. See yah!
Lexa

Journal of Sam Duffy

Day 146

I was feeling a bit blah today so I FaceTimed my sister. It was really nice! Sometimes she can really get on my nerves, but today it was good! I really need that.

Journal of Sam Duffy

Day 147

I don't get what is wrong with me, all I do is fucking cry. Like all the god damn time. Seriously I cried watching a commercial yesterday!

The thing is I hate crying, and I NEVER cry in front of someone. I never even cried in front of Martin and we dated for two years! But now I'll be watching Queer Eye with Mia and every 5 mins I'm sobbing. I don't know how this has happened??? I would be embarrassed about the crying in front of Mia thing, but she was crying as well.

Not only that but I've gained 3kgs this past 2 months. If it wasn't for my complete lack of a romantic life, I would think I'm pregnant. And now here I am crying, for no reason because somehow the relief I haven't had sex in five months is making me so happy.

Though, if there was a time your going to gain weight and look like a hermit than a fucking pandemic is that time! I keep seeing ad's and influencers talking about a lockdown glow up as if this is the perfect time to really starve ourselves and focus on what really matters - our appearance. Usually, that type of shit works on me, but right now, it just makes me SO mad! It's all a marketing ploy anyway. No one is going on dates or going to the gym or going to the beach so there's no need to strive for a 'beach body' and buy their products - so this is what they've come up with.

If anything a few kgs of extra fat is more of what we need right now. The way 2020 is going, we might just run out of food and guess who will be laughing then?? The bitches whose bodies have extra reserves to snack off, that's who. Pfft, lockdown glow up my ass.

May 2020

Journal of Sam Duffy

Day 153

The other day I was taking a long, thoughtful shower when it hit me - The Perfect Plan. Flirting with mystery window boy is so tricky, I need to find a way somehow that proves he has an interest in me other than being 'just some girl who stares at him'. Yes, I need a plan that proves whether or not I'm going crazy. So mid shampoo, just finished watching Pride and Prejudice, I was thinking about how hard it would be to flirt back in the day. Then I thought about how in those type of movies there is always someone in the drawing-room reading, and I was like 'the window guy reads'. That's when it came to me. I need to find myself a book with a large title that can be seen from his apartment. I can barely make out his features from where I sit (I thought about trying binoculars - trust me - but not too creepy). Which means for this to work, I need a bold cover page.... But all I could find in my room that fit the description were two books, 'He loves me, he loves me not' and a large hardcover copy of 'The Power of Data' (a book gifted from work). The only question is do I look like the love-obsessed freak that I am OR an intellectual goddess that I am not??

So the plan lies true and simple:

- Pretend to read 'The Power of Data'.
- Look back at him and smile, gesture to the book he is reading.
- Take a glimpse at the title of the book.
- Order his exact same book online
- Next day pretends to read such book in a subtle but yet obvious way of telling the guy 'hey I think you're cute'.
- On the third day, if he is reading the same copy of my book ....' The Power of Data' then I have my proof! If he doesn't, then I will just never walk past a window ever again.

It sounds insane but desperate times calls for desperate measures Sally. There are some pitfalls I'm worried about: such as if his book has tiny lettering on it's cover and I can't read the name, and then the whole plan turns to shit.

It should be fine!

Anyway, it's almost 9am - I got to go test my plan! *Deep breaths* Wish me luck!

Journal of Sam Duffy

Day 153

......Okay so this is what happened.
I sat down in my usual spot right next to the corridor window, with my coffee and book in hand. He wasn't there yet which was perfect - I needed it not to look stage, but effortlessly unaware.
So, I sat reading the book - a book about data and statistics, I remind you - while drinking my coffee. Thinking that for the past five minutes, he was sitting there watching me read this thing. I grab a quick look to my right, and he wasn't even there!

The day of all days he wasn't at the window dead on 9am! Not losing face I gave it another five minutes and continued reading. That five minutes came and went, and I looked back, and he still wasn't there.
I sat there feeling deflated at another one of my failed attempts to flirt when I saw a figure move into the room. Quickly I picked the book back up and continued to read. After 5 minutes, I look back to the window and give him my usual bright-but-not-too-bright-that-it-seems-over-eager-smile, and I got a smile and wave back.
(Is it utterly insane that just a small wave from a stranger I don't even know could make my stomach go all uneasy?? Honestly Dr Richards, please let me know if this is normal in your next email because I feel like this is insane having a crush on window boy).
And this is where my acting genius - not just honed and flourished in my Primary School play - made its debut.

Taking inspiration from the multitude of Romantic movies that I have watched over the years, I took up the role of 'the unsuspecting love interest'.

After our morning hello, I took a glance at his book, turned to look back at mine as if to read it and then as if just noticing, looked more obviously back at his book.
Luckily for me, he was already looking over! AND just as I was about to do my effortless and flawless enactment of 'oh what's that book your reading there?', mysterious window boy was making the gesture for me. I didn't even have to act the part of being a little bit surprised he was trying to ask me this!

I showed him the book cover of 'The Power of Data', for some reason I became really self-conscious (even though I planned this!) and I could feel myself blushing! ((God if we do go out he better not ask me any questions about data!)). Window boy seemed to read it as he did a little chuckle and nodded, admiring my taste.
I gestured back, and he pressed his book up to the window - 'Black Leopard, Red Wolf' by Marlon James. I admit I had to really squint to read the title. Maybe I need glasses??

The last few hours sitting in front of the window, I was so overwhelmed that my plan had actually worked! Well, sort of - still have to do the main experiment. But omg!! And bonus, since I couldn't just stop reading after that, I ended up reading the first 50 pages of 'The Power of Data' - my boss will be so happy!

Ekkkkkkkkk!!!

Raining Books

Hello Sam Duffy
Thank you for placing your order with us; the details are below.
We'll let you know when your order has been sent out.
Just so you know, Credit/Debit card payments are taken when your item(s) are being prepared for dispatch.

Estimated Order Delivery: 1 - 2 working days.

Total: £6.99

Title: Black Leopard, Red Wolf (The Dark Star Trilogy) (Paperback)
Author: Marlon James
Qty: 1
Price: £6.99
Availability at time of order: Usually dispatched within 24 hours

Journal of Sam Duffy

Day 154

The book hasn't arrived yet, and I missed the opportunity to enact the second stage of my plan this morning.
Would it be weird to do it two days after? Like, would find it creepy that I planned this for two days?? Omg is it fucking weird? Maybe I shouldn't do it and just forget about it before I blow whatever the fuck this is without creeping him out. Yeah no, I shouldn't do it.

On other news - my Self Care game has NEVER been so strong. Recently I got back into watching the news and doom scrolling way more than is healthy, and every now and again, I can feel the stress building, so I have been proactive!
In the morning's I make sure to eat breakfast without the news on but with cartoons (I tried not watching anything while I ate but I just got bored). Then I do 10 mins of yoga or just stretch before I get ready for work. If at any point I feel stressed I take 5 mins just to breath 4 seconds in - 4 seconds out. At lunch, I go for an hour-long walk with coffee. In the afternoons, I draw myself a bubble bath, put on music and have a glass of wine. I know what your thinking - I sound like I'm 40, but right now I'm dealing with a 40 year olds amount of stress (and I'm talking one with preteens yelling at them type of stress). And you know what I fucking love it!

Every night M and I make ourselves dinner, paint our nails or wear mud masks. I've always been too busy or had too many things to think about that I wouldn't allow myself these type of moments.

Journal of Sam Duffy

Day 155

The book arrived!! Granted it was at 7.30am but who cares - it's here! My stomach is all in knots :/
I have no idea what the fuck I'm doing - is it a good idea? Should I do it or will I come off like a crazy loser???

No no no, I can't keep overthinking. I want to know if he is interested in me, so I have to do this!....right??

Okay okay, I will let you know how it goes!

....Soooo yeah I have no fucking idea how that went! I sat down in a way that would show off my new book to Mystery boy and waited for him to notice. It didn't take long! As we were doing a morning ritual of saying hi to each other, he pointed at the book like 'is that..?" so I smiled and put it closer to the window so he could see that I was reading his book. He squinted a little to read it and then seemed slightly surprised. But I have no idea whether it was a good surprise or an 'oh god she is nuts' surprise. And then I gestured like it was an excellent read (even though I have read 5 pages so far) and he smiled really wide at that. Which could be a genuine smile of 'that was so cute, and I'm stoked she's into me', OR it could have been a 'just keep smiling because this person is deranged' type of smile.

I know I'm overthinking this but what else can I do?? I have nothing to do, and he's too far away from my line of sight to be able to correctly read his damn body behaviour.

Ahhhhhh this sucks! I thought I would feel better after doing it, but I feel worse - like my mind won't stop overthinking and every minute feels like forever because now I just can't wait for tomorrow morning so I can see if my gesture was reciprocated :(

Oh shit, what if it isn't??

5th May 2020

Dear Grandma,

Thank you for your lovely birthday wishes! ~~The letter arrived on time!~~

~~My new friends spoilt me and took me to Paris for my birthday. Unfortunately no Martin didn't propose, instead he decided to go off with some other girl from his office.~~

~~I did plan to go to Ireland! But the pandemic happened and now i'm a young thriving 24 year old, boyfriend-less, alone, sitting in only an over sized tee and undies eating her body weight in popcorn trying to numb myself~~

Journal of Sam Duffy

Day 157

Today I tried - I really did try Dr Richards - to write Granny back. But I have nothing to say! At least nothing to say that won't make her have a heart attack :(

I need to at least need to have a new boyfriend and maybe some pictures of me in Ireland before I break the news - you know sweeten the blow a little bit. Though both those things aren't happening anytime soon!

I've got her last letter cello taped to my mirror so I won't forget about it, but all it does now is fill me with deep sadness and guilt.

Oh, and Mystery Window Boy was reading the same book he was reading yesterday...so there's my question answered. It's so strange how someone you don't know, doesn't do something you've dreamed up in your head and then it depresses you for the rest of the day.

Though he did still wave and smile at me this morning instead of choosing to never sit next to his window again - so my crazy little brain is still the tiniest bit hopeful!

Journal of Sam Duffy

Day 158

When I had almost given up! When I thought all hope was lost and I was going to die a damn spinster - guess what happens!

I sat down in my usual spot this morning. Said 'hello' (a little awkwardly because at the time I thought I had been subtly rejected), and then went to go open my work emails...when something caught my eye. Sitting right next to the window was a very cute mystery boy reading my book, "The Power of Data". MY HEART! Omg, I was so happy and surprised. I felt like I had lost a full minute. He smiled up at me and chuckled, then pointed at the book with a shrug, as if to say 'eh'. I cannot wait to tell Mia!!

He bought my book!!! A fucking book about statistics - my god this guy must really be into me - or maybe it was a pity gesture so it wasn't awkward nope can't think like that BECAUSE HE LIKES ME!

I'm not going to die eaten by my own cats! This is the best thing that has happened to me in months!!

Journal of Sam Duffy

Day 160

Mia and Parker had another big fight this afternoon. Offset by Parker having to pull another all-nighter at the office.
(If I didn't know Parker or that Mia goes down to his office to check if he is actually there and working, I would suspect he was fooling around like Martin did to me. The only difference is Parker isn't Mia's Walter - those two were meant to be together.)

So I went down to Waitrose bought some wine, stopped off at PoundLand and bought some paint supplies.
The best thing you can do if 1. you've had a shitty day, 2. are pissed off, and 3. can't go out because there is rampant virus thriving outside, is to set yourself up all cosy on the ground with some pillows, chuck on some Bob Ross, pour yourself a big glass of wine.

Bob Ross is just amazing and so calm, but my god is he a damn liar 'this is easy', 'we don't make mistakes, just happy accidents'. What I painted was definitely not a happy accident, let me just tell you that. It looked like a 5-year-old painted it. How does Bob Ross make it look so easy???
Mia's painting was, of course, a damn masterpiece - my artistically talented friends piece looked exactly like Bob's! And she had more wine than me!

I told her she needs to showcase her skill and make videos on YouTube. I know she's busy working at the cafe and then working on her screenplay, but I think she would be an amazing influencer! It might even build herself a name, so when she's finished writing the screenplay, she could have more doors open for her and show it to some big companies.

M was all like 'What me?? No way! I could never do it!' but I could see in her eyes that she would love to do it! :P

Journal of Sam Duffy

Day 163

Omgomgomgomgomg! Window guy suggested a new book! Oh my god, my heart!
(It is moments like these, where I realise how fucking self-isolated and crazy I have become, that some random I've been perving at for several weeks does something like hold up a new book he's reading by the window, and I act like Harry Styles just dm'd me. Note to self: Must not lose it).

He looked so shy, bringing the new book up to the window as well! The way his hand nervously combed through his brown…blonde? (I can't tell from this distance) but oh man……I almost forgot he could see me drooling over him. Whoops.

I've already placed my order online AND paid extra for next day delivery - yeah, that's right, you could say things are getting serious. Take that, Martin. Prick.

Though, mystery window guy reads so fast! Forget rent, half of my paycheck is going to be spent on books! Though I wouldn't mind, except for the fact, I have to come up with books to recommend him!!! All I have been reading is romance novels that scream, 'Caution: this girl is lonely and will trap you inside her love dungeon'.

I need something thut is thought-provoking, while entertaining, and deep... random note: What did people do before Google???

Messages

Today 9am

GOV.UK CORONAVIRUS ALERT

Current guidelines and rules have been extended until 17/06/2020. Rules as still in place: you must stay home. More information and exemptions at **gov.uk/coronavirus** or text COVID19.

Stay at home, protect lives.

Messages

Text from M

Oh my god! I am going to lose it.

M
Read 9.05am

> Right!? Like I thought they said this virus was basically the flu, and then making it out like lockdown will only be in force for a month!
>
> Sam
> Read 9.06am

Girl, I know! And here we are like three months later..

M
Read 9.06am

> Someone at work said that it might be in place for another three months!
>
> Sam
> Read 9.07am

No way!!!

M
Read 9.07am

> Yeah! He was all like, 'get your home office all comfy because we're going to be working from home for a while'.
>
> Sam
> Read 9.08am

That's it! I am taking your advice, and I'm going to quit my shitty part-time job and try become an influencer.

M
Read 9.09am

Yes, you so should!

Sam

Read 9.11am

Like girl, you don't even know how paranoid I get interacting with customers all day. Some even refuse to wear a mask! I don't want to get sick and almost die just so I can earn £9 an hour.

M

Read 9.11am

Especially since Parker is making all this money, I shouldn't be risking my health for money we don't even need. Right?

M

Read 9.12am

Girl, is this a stupid idea?

I just think, working at the cafe during this time is putting me in a really bad mood, so when Parker isn't home to cheer me up or rant to, it makes me even sadder.

M

Read 9.20am

Sorry! Just had a quick shower!

No, honestly, my advise would be that no one should feel like they need to stay in a job or relationship or whatever, that is affecting their mental health. Also if you think this will help your relationship then it's like - do you stay in a shitty job you don't need or do you quit and focus on the only thing that matters to you right now?

Sam

Read 9.23am

Another great way to look at it is, by giving up a position you don't like or need in terms of money or career, that just frees up another spot for someone who might actually really badly need the income :)

Sam
Read 9.24am

That does make me feel better!!

M
Read 9.25am

Okay, I'm gonna quit

M
Read 9.25am

Love yah girl xx

M
Read 9.25am

Journal of Sam Duffy

Day 169

So lockdown has been extended again. I'm not surprised as people at work have been talking about how bad it is all month. But I am still so so gutted! For one thing, I won't be able to go see window boy in person for another month! And I don't know how I'm going to be able to keep my mental health up - I've already gone way downhill in personal upkeep. Who knows how many days or weeks long, my leg hair is. My face hasn't had a single dot of foundation or unmasked sunlight in weeks that I forget that our flat isn't actually haunted, and the ghost I see in the bathroom every morning is just my pale ass face staring back at me.

:(

By the time lockdown is lifted I will be Sam no longer - but Hermit Girl, attacking any man who looks at her.

Journal of Sam Duffy

Day 171

While the UK is still in lockdown, back home in New Zealand, they have come out of it fully! FULLY! They are now in lockdown 1. Which means while I'm at home meditating away the crazy, all of my friends are posting pictures of themselves hanging out with friends, going to restaurants and genuinely enjoying life.

If it wasn't for that fucker, Martin - I could be there with my friends, living it up instead of sitting in one spot for hours, feeling the elastic waistband of my sweatpants get tighter and tighter :(

Actually no. I'm a glad came. I LOVE Brighton - even now. And I can't imagine my life without Mia and Parker in it now……I wonder if they would move to New Zealand with me??

Positive thinking. Positive thinking.

Journal of Sam Duffy

Day 172

Every day after lunch, I will peer out of the window to catch a glance at Window Boy, even though no matter what, he is never at the window past 12pm. It's like a habit now. If I sit down at my desk to "work", I can't help myself to look and hope I might be able to see him again - even from a distance. I wonder where he goes after lunch?

All of this crushing on someone I know nothing about is really hindering my productivity at work. But I can't help but imagine what it would be like meeting him, what his voice sounds like, how tall he is, what he looks like - I'm picturing a young Brad Pitt or Johnny Deep. Though if he looked like either of them, he would not be wasting any of his time window flirting with some random hermit next door.

sigh

Though I do have to say, the day to day lives of my neighbours is getting more and more interesting. I'm not stalking them I swear Dr Richards!! I just happen to, you know, glance around at the other windows when Window Boy isn't in. A harmless, and very much not intentional glance at my next-door neighbours. Who just happened not to close their curtains. Anyway, I digress - What I have observed over the past couple of weeks is a lot - who knew my neighbours lived such dramatic lives?!

First off is the couple who lives just below Window Boy's floor. At first, they were very much together - cuddling on the couch, making lunch together, all in all, being overly in love and disgusting to watch. But over the past few weeks, they have had some BIG fights! And today...I haven't seen either one be in the same room as the other.
I can't imagine just moving in with someone, to then be placed into lockdown! The poor couple didn't have a fighting chance. The dissolving nature of their relationship was really heartbreaking to watch.

AND THEN THERE IS THE BOTTOM LEVEL FLAT! I'm pretty sure it's a uni flat with 4 students living there. Two girls, two boys. Very much a party flat. The kitchen is frequently used as a hot box, and there have been many mid-afternoon drinking games to pass the time. Seeing them having fun makes me so sad - I miss University days and flat parties SO much! I wish I could go back :(
Except I am not envious of what is about to happen. Soo much drama and they don't even know. So I think two of them were seeing each other on the low at the beginning of lockdown, but I see the tallest girl making out with a different flatmate each week! And, I quite often see the two men secretly holding hands and whispering in the kitchen!!! I love this flat so much. They are literally all getting with each other, and none of them knows it!.... I wonder if they will be a quadruple? Is that a thing?

Yeah, so my productivity at work hasn't been the greatest. And it's not even the distraction that is causing it. I just can't focus like I use to. It kinda feels like a cloud goes over my mind when I look at work. There is just so much going on in the world that it no longer seems important or something...I don't know. Maybe it's just working from home for so long.

Apart from that, I am doing great! Every day I wake up so excited to see Mystery Window Guy! We are up to suggesting a new book every two days! (Next time I have to remember to recommend a really really fat book to read because I don't know how much longer my bank account can handle that much book buying!?). In total, we have read 9 books! I love it! Usually, I stick to the genres I know and love, but being forced to read something I would have never have picked up has really broadened my outlook. Who knew there were so many great authors??? I HAVE to suggest some books to you Dr S! Trust me you will LOVEEE them!

Book Suggestions (From Window Boy & Myself):

- Black Leopard, Red Wolf - Marlon James
- My Sister, the Serial Killer - Oyinkan Braithwaite
- The Handmaid's Tale - Margaret Atwood
- The Vanishing Half - Brit Bennett
- Girl, Woman, Other - Bernardine Evaristo
- Where The Crawdads Sing - Delia Owens
- A Man Called Ove - Fredrik Backman
- The Guest List - Lucy Foley
- Spy Vs Assassin - C.C.R. Carter

Personal Book Suggestions:

- No Judgements - Meg Cabot
- The Boy Next Door - Meg Cabot
- The Younger Man - Zoe Foster Blake
- The Wrong Girl - Zoe Foster Blake
- Red, White and Royal Blue - Casey McQuiston
- Party of Two - Jasmine Guillory
- After You - Jojo Moyes

Journal of Sam Duffy

Day 174

I woke up today so excited! Yesterday I just finished our latest book, and it was Mystery Window Boy's turn to suggest what book we read next...except he never turned up.

Which is so strange because I literally have not seen him not sit by that window since March.

I'm sure it's nothing - it must have been an unintentional sleep in or maybe he is sick and had to go the hospital - OH I hope he's not 'sick'.

Though I can't help but wonder, though.
(Must not overthink this).

Journal of Sam Duffy

Day 175

He wasn't at the window again today!

Did he hate my last book suggestion? Omg, what if he hated all of my book suggestions and that last book was the final straw!

Or what if he was just being polite by suggesting books so the mornings wouldn't be awkward? Then finally thought "I don't care if she seems crazy - I am not keeping this up". Omg have I been unintentionally stalking and harassing my poor neighbour???

God, I must get a grip. It has only been two days without seeing him - I am just overthinking this....Right??

Journal of Sam Duffy

Day 176

OMG, I DID CREEP HIM OUT.

Three days now and he still hasn't turned up - not even to make a quick cup of tea! I have creeped him out so much with all my crazy that he feels like he can't even make a damn tea in the morning.

What has this lockdown done to me? Maybe I should move my desk?

P.S My indoor plants are dying. I can't even blame them.
Today I stared at their dropping leaves for five minutes. I have never connected with plants before, but I feel their pain. Like... "Yeah same.".

Journal of Sam Duffy

Day 177

You know what I am not even phased, if he is no longer interested in me, then I can handle that. Rejection is healthy. Sometimes it is just not meant to be!

On the upside, I no longer have to get dressed just to sit by the window, AND I can pop my pimples again without fear he will see it - which I already have. Hello, sweatpants, red marks and being carefree again.

One thing I find strange is every so often I remember our flat is right in the middle of the city. There used to be so much noise outside, from cars, foot traffic and the occasional ramblings of drunken people. Now it's dead quiet. It's nice but surreal.

Speaking of outside - I need a coffee, and a LONG walk to clear my mind - maybe I should meditate and have a bubble bath later, with wine.

Note to self: Pick up wine.

Journal of Sam Duffy

Day 177

AHHHHHHHH the worst thing that could have to happen - happened.

Okay, so I was on my way to get coffee at my local cafe when it struck me. I had been going to the same cafe for so long now, through mental breakdowns, and pimple breakouts, that I almost forgot there was a hot barista who serves me every day. Realising this, the anxiety washed over me. I could not go and see the hot barista with freshly popped pimples and sweatpants. Sure he had seen me like this before but not since I started wearing real clothes for window guy. So I decided, just for today, I will try to find a new cafe.

Little did I know that the cafe I was headed to was Hot Barista Guy's local. I didn't even recognise him when I lined up outside! It's not like I have ever seen him out in the wild before. But man is he beautiful. Those cheekbones...the tattoos..the jaw you could fucking cut butter with! So guess my shock when the guy, standing exactly two metres in front of me turns around, and I realise in pure shock and horror that it was him! And he was talking to me! I looked like a crypt keeper or something. I could feel my face burn red from embarrassment.

Once I got over the initial shock, I was surprised that he was easy to talk to. I don't know if it's the lack of social contact, but he seemed like he really wanted to keep talking. I mean he got his coffee first and stuck around to talk to me while I ordered and waited for mine. And then was still talking to me when I grabbed my coffee. So strange...surely he has an equally godlike girlfriend back at his flat or could have - why would he be talking to a pimple popping loser like me??

I don't know why but when he leaned back against the side of the coffee shop, talking about...what was he talking about???...anyway I couldn't help but stare at his hands. They were so tan and strong, I could help imagine my deathly white fingers wrapped up in his. AND THAT'S WHEN I REALISED HE HAD STOPPED TALKING AND NOTICED ME STARING AT HIS FINGERS. Like omg, why am I such a weirdo? And if you're thinking 'oh you can still recover from that', then you are right I COULD have, but did I?? No, no, I did not. Instead, I panicked, told him I to be somewhere (like bitch where would I have to go - during a lockdown??), and fled the scene.

Oh god. Why do I do this to myself?

Journal of Sam Duffy

Day 178

It's 1.30pm - the usual time I go for a midday walk and coffee. Window boy was still a no show, and the anxiety of going to the coffee shop again is a definite no.

God how weird I acted staring at his hands, looking a mess - it's too embarrassing. I don't know if I can handle seeing the barista suddenly cower away from me, especially after window boys sudden rejection.

Definitely have to avoid coffee shop from now.

I also feel weirdly guilty about crushing on barista guy when I was just crushing on Mystery Window Guy. Like what insane person likes two guys - she barely knows - at the same time, while also thinking both gorgeous men have a crush on her too?

I really really need to stop reading romantic novels. It's giving me unrealistic expectations. Also, maybe I should take Lex's suggestion and do a Zoom date??

Journal of Sam Duffy

Day 180

I opened my 2020 year planner this morning for the first time in months. It is so depressing to look - I had forgotten what this year was like before and what it was meant to be.

Here are some of my goals:
- Expel Martin from my life! (This one - I'm at least doing well on)
- Save enough money to travel (pointless)
- Travel to Paris, Morocco, Ireland, Scotland, Italy, Greece, Croatia, the Netherlands. :(:(
- Listen to Feminist Podcasts. (Currently listening to them!)
- Loose 5 kgs (hahaha)
- Become hot aka GLOW UP (...)
- Get a hot new boyfriend (This one just hurts)
- Read Feminist Lit (...kind of)
- If it's less than an hour away - walk (aka stop being a lazy bitch). (If only I had realised the luxury of walking).
- Go to flat parties and clubs on the beach :(
- Learn how to surf or/& skateboard :(
- Pride Week/Carnival Brighton!!!! (Has been cancelled)

Journal of Sam Duffy

Day 181

"I'm bored in the house, I'm in the house bored. Bored in the house, bored in the house, bored."

I cannot get that song out of my head. It's so damn relatable and catchy.

"I'm bored in the house, I'm in the house bored. Bored in the house, bored in the house, bored."

To: Sam.Duffy@aol.com

From: Prof.Duffy@aol.com

Subject: Your Grandma

Hi honey,

I hope you are surviving okay in the UK's extended lockdown. It won't be forever.

Though, I do want you to write back to your poor Grandmother. I get calls from her every day asking how you are and how she hasn't heard back from you. Really Samantha, is it that hard to write a letter?

Thinking of you,
Mum xxxoo

June 2020

Journal of Sam Duffy

Day 183

It's officially summer!!

Yesterday I tried going to the beach for my midday walk, and the whole beach was packed full of people. Apparently, when it's 30 degrees, no one cares that there is a deadly virus going around. Though I can't blame them too much - the UK doesn't seem to have air-cons in any flat! At home, I have been having to put ice packs on my feet just to stop from getting heatstroke. Anyway - since I can no longer go for a beach walk at midday, I decided today I will be getting up early to go on the walk before work instead. But bloody hell, it was already over 20 degrees at 7am this morning. It felt like walking into a sauna! And to my disbelief, there were so many people out by the beach. I think everyone who usually goes for a walk or jog later on in the day had the same idea as me and decided to go early morning. Except there was no way I was risking walking through sweaty, unsocially distanced crowds. Nah ah, I'm going to find a new walking track.
It's put me in such a sad mood all day. I love summer and going to the beach but when you're stuck inside - forced to sweat to death - it sucks!

And then throw in having to find a new route, when your old one was basically perfect, it just sucks.

The major problem with finding a new walking track is there are hardly any. That is unless I want to walk up steep hills for an hour - which let's be honest, I might do it once, but a bitch too lazy to do it on the regular.

:(

Journal of Sam Duffy

Day 186

Today is the day I face my fear and go back to my favourite cafe. It's just ridiculous this sudden fear I have after breaking up with Martin. It's like I think I'm no longer good enough for anyone I find attractive. Like FUCK THAT. Why should I punish myself like this - I did nothing wrong. And you know what...I am cute! And nice and funny and smart. I can get any guy I want!

I just got to get hold of this fucking anxiety. Why is anxiety so irrational. You get all these thoughts at the time that make you cower in fear and run away, but once you're home 'safe' away from people - it's like 'what the fuck?! What was I thinking - it was totally fine!'.

So that's what I'm going to do. Tell my anxiety to shut the fuck up, face hot barista boy and flirt!

Journal of Sam Duffy

Day 187

Update: I went to the cafe, and everything went really well! I was flirting, making him laugh while he made me coffee. I was killing it! I had gotten my fucking flirting game back....And then I took a sip of my coffee. He gave me Oat milk. OAT MILK.

The thing is - I come here almost every day, order the same coffee. And he even calls me Mocha girl. So I was like oh maybe I picked up the wrong order. I went back up to the cafe window and said I must have grabbed someone else's coffee as this has oat milk in it. And he looked at me so confused saying "Oh I thought you always got Oat milk". My heart exploded. I was so embarrassed to think this god-like man actually liked me or like noticed me - so I said 'Ah no, usually just normal milk. But that's fine - it actually tastes good. Just didn't want to have stolen someone else's order.".

To be fair, he was really really nice about it and apologetic, and tried hard for me to let him make a new coffee - but my face was burning red, and I HAD to get out of there.

Sigh

I am back to finding a new cafe. But it might work out since I have to find a new walking track anyway!

Journal of Sam Duffy

Day 190

Today I am moving my desk! I think it will be extremely healthy for me.

After mystery window guy and the hot barista, I have to retrain my brain. I am now no longer allowed to fantasise and daydream - I will be focused on reality and have very structured and productive days.

The first step: is moving my desk into my room, so I can't be distracted by what is happening in the lives of my neighbours, or depressed at the absence of Window Boy.

The desk will just fit in my bedroom, but it will be good for me! Healthy.

A new, healthy and productive Sam.

Face-to-Face

11:22pm 11/06/20

Lexa Duffy | Online

Call Connecting

Long time, no see.
_{Lexa}

> How's the lockdown-free life?
> _{Sam}

Ah so good! I went for a bike ride yesterday and then went for brunch with friends.
_{Lexa}

> You went for brunch! Omg, I almost forgot about brunch. Tell me what you got so I can live through you.
> _{Sam}

Haha, I'll send you a photo, but I got crepes with berries and a small scoop of vanilla ice-cream on top. And do you know how they sometimes give you a small jug of maple syrup for pancakes?
_{Lexa}

> Yeahhh
> _{Sam}

Well, it came with one of those little jugs, but instead of maple syrup, it was melted chocolate!
_{Lexa}

> You bitch! Arghhh I'm so jealous, it's so unfair.
> _{Sam}

Hehe yeah, it was good! How is life in Brighton at the moment? Have you thought about doing that Zoom dating I was telling you about?
Lexa

Life at the moment is very 'same same'. Work is fine. But it's getting so hot here! And yes I have been thinking about going on a Zoom date. It sounds awful! But....I may try it out.
Sam

Omg yes! Please tell me how it goes! I am so curious.
Lexa

Haha you know you could always try it out yourself.
Sam

Ew no! I mean I can't, I have a boyfriend.
Lexa

How is that going by the way? Do you Looovvve him yet?
Sam

hehe maybe...
Lexa

Oh my god! Have you told him that?
Sam

No! It's only been like six months. And I want to wait until he says it first.
Lexa

Why's that? Do you not think he is in love with you yet or something?
Sam

Nah I'm pretty sure he is. He told me a couple weekends ago at a flat party that he loved me. But I'm worried he was just really drunk.
Lexa

Aw, you love each other! If he said it when he was drunk, then he means it. People always say what they mean when they're drunk. Plus if you love someone...let them know.

Sam

Ekk okay... I might. I gotta go, but we should video call more often!
Lexa

Yeah, we should! Alright, see yah.

Sam

Journal of Sam Duffy

Day 193

My new walk is amazing! To bypass the beach and hills on my new walking route, I decided to go through the city centre and explore all the different alleyways and lanes that I haven't seen yet.
And holy shit there are so many different lanes in the city! I almost got lost at one point.

The best part of my new route is all the cats I see out and about!
There are so many, and they look so cute and cuddly!! I wish I could pat them SO badly - but I don't know if that is allowed nowadays. Like what if I pat the cat and she/he has germs that make me sick or vice versa.

Though I can still look at their cute little chubby faces!
There are two cats on one street that are super friendly. A thin but very clean tabby comes out from beneath parked cuddles and meows and walks through my legs to get pats. And then there is this big chubby white cat that is always dirty, with matted fur, that sleeps in a different garden every day, basking in the sun.
Just a street away from those two cuties is a thin alleyway with three more cats - but they aren't very sociable. One of these days, they will love me. And I will get those damn pats!

Journal of Sam Duffy

Day 194

I went out this morning with Mia to get some pink hair dye and wine. It was really nice hanging out with her again. Ever since she quit her job at the cafe, she has been going hard with creating content for her new YouTube channel. I love it so much. She seems really happy and finally passionate about her work. I mean M is crazy creative and charismatic, it just makes so much sense for her to do this than be stuck in a job with no creativity in it at all.

Plus Parker and Mia seem to be doing a lot better. I have noticed a real lack of yelling in the morning, and a lot more inappropriate groping in public spaces (which I very much do not appreciate).

While bleaching and then dying Mia's long black hair pink, she was telling me how they had a big talk a few days ago to sort everything out, and to see things from both perspectives. Parker has talked to his boss FINALLY, saying that he had to have at least one day off a week and work no more than 10 hours of work a day. I mean....to me it still doesn't sound great, but as long as M can see Parker at least for a few hours a day is really really good. Mia even said he got the last two weeks of July off, which is awesome!!

I'm glad they are not breaking up! Not just because I love those two so much, and they are such a cute couple, but holy shit how awful would it be having to be self-isolating with two people who just broke up after like 6 years?!

To: Sam.Duffy@aol.com

From: Prof.Duffy@aol.com

Subject: Grandma

Darling,

I have some terrible news. I am so sorry honey to be letting you know through email, but I have no other way to get hold of you.

Sweetheart, I got a phone call this morning from the retirement village. Granny passed away last night.

She had a beautiful life and knew all of us loved her very much.
The funeral is in two days, as you know it will be quite a small gathering because of all the current restrictions.

Oh, Sweetheart, I am so sorry you had to hear it this way.

I love you very much and hope your okay!
Mum
xxxxoooo

Bank Account

Balance £2353

Overdraft Available £2853

Air Aotearoa

London → New Zealand

Total price from
£2,500

Sunday, 14th June	21:00	35hr	1 Stop (7hrs)
Air Aotearoa	Departure	LGW-NZ	Hong Kong Int Airport

1 Free Carry On   1 Checked On Bags

To: Sam.Duffy@aol.com

From: Air.Aotearoa.AirAo.com

Subject: You're booking with Air Aotearoa…

Your booking is confirmed.

Booking reference: H0EJABH

Kia ora SAMANTHA DUFFY,

Thanks for booking your trip with us.

We just wanted to let you know, due to special circumstances, Hong Kong International Airport is not allowing transit passengers at this time. Our team is looking into when the restriction will be lifted and will alert you as soon as we know.

You can find all of this information and more online at AirAotearoa.co.nz.

If you would like to rebook your flight or receive a refund on this flight, please email us and let us know.

Journal of Sam Duffy

Day 195

I don't even know how to write this....
I can't stop crying, I can't even bring myself to tell work.
Losing someone, I loved while being overseas was not what I thought would have ever have happened. I don't have any family around me, and I feel so alone.

I tried getting a flight out for tonight, so I could get back in time for the funeral, but the flight has been cancelled, and I have no idea when transits will opening up again.

I have never felt trapped before. I can't leave even if I had a million dollars.

I don't know what to do.

I feel so guilty. I was so fucking selfish and stupid. I should have written back to her. And now I can't attend her funeral.

I really want to be there, to mourn, to properly say goodbye. But I'm stuck here, alone.

I'm so so so sorry Granny. I love you.

Face-to-Face

10:00pm 14/06/20

Lexa Duffy | Online

Call Connecting
Call Failed

Face-to-Face

10:20pm 14/06/20

Lexa Duffy | Online

Call Connecting
Call Failed

Messages

Lex: Sam please pick up.

Face-to-Face

10:52pm 15/06/20

Lexa Duffy | Online

Call Connecting
Call Failed

Messages

Lex: I'm worried about you.

To: Sam.Duffy@aol.com

From: Richards.Sally@London.ac.uk

Subject: Next week's entires

Hi Samantha,

Thank you for sending through last week's diary entries.

I wanted to give you my condolences for your loss and to let you know I don't expect any diary entries this week.

Everyone grieves in their own way. I hope this helps you grieve in yours.

Sincerely,

Sally.

Messages

Text from M

Hey girl, I've noticed you haven't come out of your room for a while. I hope you're okay. If you want to talk about it, I'm just a yell away xxx

M
Read 12.02am

Heyy, I have left a plate of dinner just outside your door if you're hungry. And there is also a wee box of goodies that might help you feel better xxx

M
Read 7.13pm

I love you. If you need just someone to cry to, I'm always here and so is Parker xoxo

M
Read 5.55pm

Journal of Sam Duffy

Day 200

I got out of bed today. Made breakfast.

Work has let me have two weeks off, paid. Which is really nice of them.

Mia and Parker have been so thoughtful. Every day they put a plate of food just outside my door. I don't feel like I deserve it.

I feel a little bit numb and tired.

Is it strange that I haven't cried since I found out, that I just sleep instead??

I hate myself for being here and not back home.

Journal of Sam Duffy

Day 202

Mia caught me making breakfast today. I hadn't realised I was hiding from her until then, I guess I just didn't want to talk about it. Not straight away.

Though it was nice letting her in, talking about it. I forget she is away from her home country too. She understands. It seems weird how just knowing someone close to you does the simple thing of understanding your pain, helps, even slightly.

I took a shower today. It was the best thing I have done all week. I didn't get out until the water went cold.
I might do it again tomorrow.

Journal of Sam Duffy

Day 204

Every day I wake up at 10.30am now and go grab breakfast, and every time Mia is there waiting for me with a cup of coffee.
She sits down as I make my food, and just talks to me, about anything and everything. The more stupid and ridiculous the better - to try and get me to laugh, to get my mind off of it, I think.

I really love M. I don't what I would do without her or how I deserve such a beautiful friend.

This morning I decided to sit down with her in the lounge instead of eating breakfast in my room. We talked for hours. It was nice. I feel so much lighter.
And she's right if granny could see me now, inside and unkept for days instead of all dolled up and out looking for my future husband, she would be so upset.

For Granny, I will start...I guess living again. At least I will try to until it gets easier.

Journal of Sam Duffy

Day 204

Parker got time off work tonight, as I think a not so secret plan put in force by Mia to have a flat movie night, to try and cheer me up.

I love those two!

They let me pick what we would watch, and I'm a massive sucker for a good Zombie movie! And so we watched one. But um, woah, what a big mistake that was.

Tip: Don't watch Zombie movies...or deadly virus movies or natural disaster movies during a pandemic.

Like damn, do they hit different. Usually, I love Zombie movies because it's a little bit scary and silly and just so entertaining. But watching it now - holy crap that shit was like bone-chilling. That shit just doesn't feel so far fetched anymore, or silly, like after what happened this year - who fucking knows what could happen.

10th June, 2020

Hello, my darling Samantha,

I'm not sure if you got my last letter. Hopefully, it wasn't lost in the mail.

I just wanted to write and see how you are doing? I hate thinking of you being all alone in that big city, so away from home. Your mother assures me you are fine and are perfectly capable of looking after yourself. I'm sure that is true, Samantha, but as I told your mother, it does not stop me from worrying about my favourite granddaughter.

Well, my darling girl, please do look after yourself, and if you need any help don't even think twice about letting your granny know! I would be flying over to pick you up now if it wasn't for my bung knees.

Write back soon,

Ta ta for now,

Love,

Granny xx

July 2020

Journal of Sam Duffy

Day 228

Today I woke up to the sounds of restless feet pouring down the street. People, with the government's guidance, have gone back to wandering through the streets, grabbing take away coffee - generally just spoiling an introverts heaven.

I miss when the streets were barren, no one in sight - absolutely nothing around to cause my social anxiety to flare up. It was so lovely! Now I can feel it creeping back in, but worse because now I have the additional fear of their germs.

The government has now allowed all shops - except tattoo parlours and movie theatres - to open back up, with socially distant guidelines of course. People are also allowed to hang out with no more than 5 people, outdoors for picnics. Which is more than enough for me - I only hang out with two other people.

Though this does open up to the possibility of meeting someone again :)

Messages

Text from M

Girl, are you up yet?
M
Read 10.05am

…Possibly.
Sam
Read 9.06am

Yay perfect! I was thinking we could go for for a bike ride :P
M
Read 10.05am

Ahhh, oh yeah, shit I can't - don't have a bike sorry!
Sam
Read 9.06am

That is no problem! We can just hire one.
M
Read 10.05am

Sam is typing

Oh, come on Sam! It will be fun, I swear!
M
Read 10.05am

It's only a 30 min bike ride to this cute little seaside village, and we can have a small picnic with wine!
M
Read 10.05am

Hmm, I don't know M. I t's meant to be 33 degrees today, and biking up hills is not something I want to do in that heat.

Sam
Read 9.06am

…there is only a slight, tiny winy, hill!

M
Read 10.05am

Hahaha no.

Sam
Read 9.06am

I'll buy you a coffee :P

M
Read 10.05am

Fuck you

Sam
Read 9.06am

I'll be ready in five :(

Sam
Read 9.06am

Yay!!!

M
Read 10.05am

Journal of Sam Duffy

Day 231

Oh my god, my vagina!!
You know those adorable music videos or rom-coms of girls going out on a cute as fuck bike ride? Yeah well, what they don't show is the girl barely able to walk the next day because the bike seat has bruised her downstairs!
I knew there was a reason I didn't like bike riding.

....though apart from the inability to walk without pain "thing" - I had so much fun. M, as always, was right. Just biking through town was so exhilarating, I felt so free for the first time in months!
We went to this small seaside town, and it was beautiful. They had pubs made 200 years ago with tiny little door frames - because people were a lot smaller back then!! Amazing! Even though we didn't go that far out, it was nice to get that sense of 'travelling'/exploring back again.

Though my fucking vagina is paying the price for it! :(

I have also decided to resume my daily walks! I think it's about time I force myself back into a daily ritual and to get into fresh clothes every morning. Plus who knows who I might bump into, now that everyone's allowed back out! :P

I was also thinking...even though girls are now dressing up again and wearing makeup - I might stay make up free for a while. Maybe. I'll try at least :/

Messages

Text from Don't Answer

I miss you
Don't Answer
Read 12.50am

I can't stop thinking about you. What I did.
Don't Answer
Read 1.24am

Do you think we could meet up again? I can shout coffee.
Don't Answer
Read 1.35am

Messages

Text M

Argh gross! Guess who texted me last night?
Sam
Read 6.43am

Hmm… let see. Late night text. Didn't see it until apparently now, which is 6.45am Samantha! So I go with your ex?
M
Read 6.45am

…damn. Yeah.
He wants to get 'coffee'.
Sam
Read 6.46am

EW! Shall we Sunday Drunk, Bake & Bitch?!
M
Read 6.47am

Thought you would never ask! ♡
Sam
Read 6.47am

Journal of Sam Duffy

Day 235

I have had the BEST day!

Bloody karma is a damn bitch babyyyy

Just knowing Martin is over in London, stuck in a flat for months on end with a girl he barely knows, missing me and regretting ever letting me go - is the best fucking gift I could have asked for!!

And there is NO WAY I am getting coffee with him after what he did, how he treated me like nothing, and not even sending me a text after my granny passed!

I can't believe I let him make me feel less than or unworthy of love. After being cheated on and left for a completely different type of woman - I had like no self-confidence - NONE!

Arghh fuck him.

I don't even feel bad that I'm enjoying his misery so much!

Though I do regret all the cupcakes and wine, I just had :/ Oops.

Journal of Sam Duffy

Day 236

I may have... accidentally...patted some cats today. They are just so cute! and I see them every damn day, and they look SO sad when I don't pat them! I had to do it! I just had to.

Though I was very responsible about it. Before and after patting, I sanitised my hands. So I covered all bases.

I also went into The Lanes today and picked up a few pieces from a little local boutique that sells all of these cool indie, one of a kind pieces of clothing. I haven't been shopping in so long, it was so nice. And also very important to support small businesses, especially now.

I have been living in my old grungy clothes for so long, I forgot how nice it is to wear cute outfits! I went from looking like Britney Spears when she shaved her head to Britney spears in her 2016 music video - Toxic. I feel damn fine and brand new.

P.s you may be thinking - why did you not just buy clothes online during lockdown?? - and I will tell you why. I'm 5ft10, with DD's... online shopping is SO hard. Either the dresses barely cover my bum, or my boobs can't fit.

Journal of Sam Duffy

Day 238

At the moment, the UK government has enforced people to wear masks inside shops and whenever possible unless walking outside and eating at restaurants. Which I have already been doing for my weekly supermarket shops, but since the streets are becoming SO packed full of people again, I have been wearing my mask as soon as I get outside.

I am so grateful for masks, and for the protection it gives us from you know...the plague.

But omg do I have some qualms with them.

1st - My breath just gets trapped in the fabric, so not only do I smell my breath for the first few minutes, the lower half of my face becomes uncomfortable, hot and sweaty :(
2nd - I can't tell if someone is a.hot and b.looking at me in a 'why hello there' type of way, or if it's a, 'ew look at that weirdo' look.

When you thought flirting and finding a bloody date was hard enough, they just have to go and enforce masks!

~~2020 - year of Sam~~

Journal of Sam Duffy

Day 239

Do you remember Dr R how I may have started giving my neighbourhood's cats a few, well deserved, pats?

Well, while on my walk today, I passed by the chubby white cat who's fur is always matted and dirty, only now it's fur is clean and had been brushed!

I mean it's not that strange, maybe it's owner finally got around to bathing it. Except that thought was quickly unravelled when I went to go pat the cat (after sanitising my hands), a middle-aged woman came out of her house and just stood there, watching me with stink eye!

So...there were no cat cuddles today. I don't blame the lady for getting pissed off at me, I do understand where she's is coming from, but I am just a bit sad today knowing I won't be able to pat the neighbourhoods cats anymore :'(

...~~Maybe I could lure them to my place with treats and keep them as my own~~ haha just kiddy Dr R!

Journal of Sam Duffy

Day 240

Today is the day I have forced myself to be courageous, to take the plunge into the unknown and go on a zoom date with a complete stranger.

I will go into it completely open-minded!

It will be fine.

Zoom

Luke M | Online   6:30pm 30/07/20

Call Connecting

> Hi, how you?
> Sam

Hey, I'm good. You're very pretty.
Luke

> Oh, thank you - I don't know about that...
> Sam

No...you're gorgeous, really gorgeous.
Luke

> Haha thanks. You're not so bad yourself.
> Are you okay? You seem to be breathing quite heavily.
> Sam

Mmm I'm good.
Luke

> ...is that...your penis?
> Oh my god are you wanking?!
> Sam

Call Ended

Journal of Sam Duffy

Day 240

~~Today is the day I have forced myself to be courageous, to take the plunge into the unknown and go on a zoom date with a complete stranger.~~

~~I will go into it completely open-minded!~~

~~It will be fine.~~

Fuck Zoom dates!

Argh yuck!

Journal of Sam Duffy

Day 241

Holllllly crap

I saw Mystery Window Boy again!!
Weirdly this morning I woke up super early, at 4am and just couldn't get back to sleep, so I decided I would get ready and go for a walk. By 5 am I showered and dressed, about to head outside, when in the corridor I chanced a look back through the window. And that's when I saw him! He was just leaving the kitchen when he quickly disappeared again. I was in complete shock at sighting this man again, after so many weeks, that I just waited for him to re-emerge in front of his kitchen window. And then out of the corner of my eye, I catch this blur. Only when I look down, the blur is window boy making his way across the street!! At that distance, I could at least make out some details about him. Very tall - taller than me - lean, with some muscle, and short black hair. But I couldn't see his face because of the stupid mask he was wearing :(

I wanted to go out and run after him, maybe get his number or something but I got too in my head if that was creepy/weird? Should I try to catch him outside next time?? He was wearing this unique black mask with red straps - maybe I can like, locate him on the street next time and like 'bump' into him...

August 2020

Journal of Sam Duffy

Day 242

I missed my alarm!! Fuck!
I was meant to wake up at 4am just like yesterday - get ready and be out the door, just in time to 'bump' into mystery window boy.
But it's 8.15 am!

I may still be able to see him. Plan B: Extremely alert daily walk. On my walk today, I am just going to be Eagle-eyed, watching out for any tall guy, with black hair and wearing a black mask with red straps!

Either that or try again tomorrow!

Journal of Sam Duffy

Day 244

Why is it so hard to just wake up early??
The past two days, I have either, slept through my alarm, or forgot to set it. And today I wake up at 4am, shower, get all cute and get ready to leave when Window Boy isn't there.
I mean it is Saturday - maybe he doesn't leave early on Saturday's?

Why is it that I can't wake up early, even when it's to weirdly stalk a guy that lives across from me?? Maybe I'm self-sabotaging? That's a thing, right? I mean, I'm nervous about bumping into him. I have been obsessing about what the fuck I will say to him other than "Hey! You're the hot guy I've been perving at all lockdown. I thought you might be here - you know on the count that I've been stalking you.".

Journal of Sam Duffy

Day 245

Ekkkkk!

Alright alright, let me set the scene.

It's 10.30am on a Sunday. I go to make a big brunch for the flat, for all they did for me last month, but to my shock, the pantry and fridge were almost barren! Thankfully Mia and Parker rarely wake up before midday on Sunday's, so I still had time to go to the supermarket, come back and make breakfast without them knowing it.

Now that things are opening up again - including pubs, the general public is back to Saturday drinks and Sunday hangovers which was perfect! I LOVE when the supermarket is like a ghost town. So already I was in a great mood without a care in the world.

And that's when I saw him. As I was about to slide open the freezer door and grab myself a bag of Hash browns - I look up and there standing... I would say 3 metres away, just on the other side of the freezer was a tall, dark and handsome man in a black mask staring at me. I froze. I was not meant to find window boy this way - I was meant to wear a cute outfit and have done my hair! Not sweatpants, singlet and messy bun!

Realising I was staring at him, I looked away, grabbed my hash browns and as I looked back up the guy was still staring.

The only fucking thing is the bloody masks! I had no idea if he was checking me out, staring like a creep or looking at something stuck to me. Thank god he realised this too because the next second he did a small wave. Hands awkwardly full of eggs, bacon and hash browns I nodded back.
"Hey, I'm Nathan!"
"Hey, hi, I'm Sam" (...I wonder if he could hear me through the mask? I like couldn't pull it down because I had no spare arms).
"Nice to meet you, Sam. I'm guessing you're making breakfast?" he nodded at what I was holding and looked back at me, "Is that for your boyfriend?"
Fucking smoooooth.
"Nah, for my flatmates. Kinda as a thank you for putting up with me during lockdown."
"haha, in that case, I should be making my flatmates a five-course meal."
He's funny!!
"So I know this is a bit forward, having just said the world's worst joke. But would you like to take a walk with me sometime? Two metres apart, of course!"
Umm yeah, I said yes like almost instantly - kinda embarrassingly fast. Though I wish I hadn't. As when he came around to give his phone number, I noticed his face mask. Black straps, I repeat black straps - not red! Not Mystery Window Boy after all.

I know, it's ridiculous not be interested in a really cute man, who is obviously interested in you, just because he isn't some mystery guy. Especially when the mystery guy is at this point, just an over fantasied person who will probably never meet my already high expectations. But I can't have three crushes - supermarket guy, barista, and window guy. No way - can't handle that much. Plus if I do go out with him, I will just always wonder about the guy across the street.

I just have to know who Window Guy is and if he is interested. If he isn't, then I can (probably cry a lot) move on.

And I would still have supermarket guy's number!

Face-to-Face

11:02pm 4/08/20

Lexa Duffy | Online

Call Connecting

> Hey!
> Sam

Finally you answer my call.
Lexa

I'm sorry! I am really. I just couldn't talk to anyone - especially not family. I would have gotten pity, or asked a billion questions, trying to think up a way I could come home and attend the funeral - when I had already come to the startling conclusion that it wasn't possible.
Sam

I understand that. But did you not think, oh hey maybe my older sister might need someone to talk to - that isn't mum.
Lexa

> No...I guess that hadn't occurred to me. Aw, Lex, I'm so sorry - I should have called and I will next time. I swear!
> Sam

Mmm okay, I forgive you, but hopefully, there won't be a next time!
Lexa

> Argh true that.
> So, how is it back home?
> Sam

It's okay. Mum is still a bit sad and overly dramatic and soppy about everything. But that should hopefully fade.
Lexa

> Haha I can just imagine!

How's the boyfriend?
Sam

He is good! He told me he loved me the other week!
Lexa

Omg, that's amazing!
Sam

Yeah, AND we are moving in together next week!
Lexa

Woah, next week? But haven't you two only been together for like 8 months?
Sam

Yes, but I have a really good feeling about it!
Honestly Sam, it will be fine! Don't give me that look - I know what I'm doing, just trust me.
Lexa

Okay okay. As long as you know the risks. I just don't like thinking of you moving in with some guy I haven't even met!
Sam

You have plenty of time to meet him when you get back home. I promise, you can judge him as much as you want when you get back.
Lexa

You swear?
Sam

Haha pinky swear. Now get some sleep!
Lexa

Goodnight.
Sam

Call Ended

Journal of Sam Duffy

Day 250

I decided this morning that I will go back to my local cafe. I mean it's just silly that I stopped going to my favourite cafe just because of a stupid crush and a little bit of oat milk. I mean he just might have had a bad day - he never got my order wrong before, and so I decided to hide from the place??

Plus I walk past it every day, and I feel so guilty. Like what if they think I don't like their coffee or them personally and would rather drink some other cafe's coffee. I'm a total coffee whore. I have been cheating on my favourite cafe with some coffee shop that's not half as good. Well, it is going to go on no longer!

Okay, I'm going to go now.

Eek, hopefully, they don't hate me now!

God, I'm ridiculous I know....anyway, I'm going!

Journal of Sam Duffy

Day 250

I'm back! And they don't hate, and everything was fine!
My god, I am my worst enemy.

I went into the store, and the girl was serving me this time. I thought fair enough, maybe hot barista boy doesn't want to serve a coffee cheater. Anyway, I got my usual and went to wait at the back of the cafe, but there were so many customers, I had to wait just in front of the coffee machine, awkwardly watching the hot barista make my order. I felt so awkward at first! Trust me if it wasn't raining, I would have just waited outside instead. But no, I had to face the awkwardness. And I'm kinda glad I did! Because I think he was flirting with me - I'll try and depict the dialogue as best I can - so please let me know if a. I'm still crazy, or b. he was definitely flirting.

Okay so.
The barista was talking to another customer as I got there, but as he gave the guy his coffee, he looked at me and smiled. I said, "Hey, how are you doing?"
"Yeah, really good! I haven't seen you in here as often?" He replied, holding my gaze.
"Oh yeah, I've been trying to test out the other cafes that are opening up again, but as you can tell I tend to stick with the cafe I like."

"haha well, I'm glad you came back. I've seen you around Bond St quite a bit getting coffee down there." He said, looking back down at the coffee machine.

"Oh, have you? Sorry, I didn't see you!"

"No, that's all good. I've actually been working there for a few weeks now."

"Really? How come I haven't seen you down there?"

"Ah, I do the awkward morning shifts no one wants to take. It's a little bit hectic as I'm never at home anymore as I work there in the early morning and here the rest of the day." He smiled back up at me.

"Shit, you must be so tired. Why did you take on the two jobs?"

"Well, I kind of wanted to show the owner down there my impeccable coffee skills so he might hire me full time... And then I will be a lot closer, and I could see you more." He said, nervously combining his fingers through his hair.

I think I froze for a few seconds from the shock of his words. Was he implying he took another job in the hopes to see more of me??

"That'd be really nice! I'm sure the owner was just as big a fan as I am of your coffee?"

His smile grew. I didn't realise I had that much effect on him. Maybe it's a barista thing, like a needed ego boost when someone compliments their coffee?

"Yeah, he did! As of next week, I will be working there from now on."

"Then I will make sure to only go to Bond St for coffee then."

He looked back up at me, like....really looked at me, and smiled. I forgot to breathe for a second. Like, what the fuck was happening? And then he passes me my coffee and says "Mocha, with no Oat milk, I promise.".

Um yeah so I couldn't remember the walk home, but as soon as I got in I had to write about this!!

What the hell just happened. Am I imagining this or was that flirting?

I just told Mia what happened - she says 'it's totally flirting'.

Omg omg! Hot barista boy likes me! I feel like a teenager again. What had 2020 done to me?!

But this just baffles my whole mind. He is so extremely hot, probably serves cute females all day. And yet he likes me?
He has seen me in like every state! When I've been depressed, anti-social, too social, all of my lockdown stages that no human should have to see. It doesn't make sense.
Apparently, Mia says it's a really good sign - she did this with Parker. When they first started dating, she wanted to cut the fat quick - to weed out fuck boy from husband material. So, she made sure to pig out on food in front of him, never wore makeup or got dressed up on dates, and invited him over when she was having period cramps, to see how he would respond. And Parker passed her test - obviously.

I guess she makes a good point. If he likes me in this state, fuck is he going to love me all done up. And, I guess, I do feel oddly comfortable around him because of it. Like with Martin, I was always so self-conscious, it was always at the back of my head, like do I look alright? Is my make up smudging? But when I talk to the barista guy (fuck why didn't I get his name?) I forget what I look like - but in a great way.

This year is so so strange.

Journal of Sam Duffy

Day 251

I woke up so early this morning. I'm just so excited to see him again! Obviously, I couldn't go straight away, that would look way too keen. Instead, I got ready. Even though I couldn't suddenly put on makeup, and wear a ball gown to see him. I did put on a little bit of mascara, perfume and a cute dress...

And then I had to watch 'Dawson's Creek' until it was an appropriate time to go get coffee.

I passed the cafe on my walk. I was walking and the closer I got, the more nervous I got. And I forgot where I was walking because I was thinking about what I would say or act when I next saw him, so I ended up at the beach. But it was actually fine! Almost no one was out as it was overcast, looking to become a downpour. Obviously, not to look too keen, I took my time wandering the beach.

Though! Unexpected twist - guess what I find on the pavement on my way back to the cafe?! A mask. But not just someone's old abandoned mask, but a black mask with red straps!

Honestly, thinking back now, I don't know why I took it. I mean it's fucking nasty to pick up anything off the ground, especially a mask during a pandemic!

At the time I was thinking, 'oh maybe I can find the owner' aka mystery window boy. Which is also stupid when just seconds ago I was obsessing about a hot barista that I actually might have a chance with.....

Anyway, I digress, I picked up the mask with two fingers and walk back to the cafe. Again the girl served me today, which I can't lie was a bit sad not to have the guy serve me. Anyway (sorry), I order my usual, when she looks down at my hand and squints.
"Where did you get that mask?"
"Oh, ah, I found it on the ground. Which is obviously very gross, but I thought the owner might have lost it and might need it. So if you know anyone around here that usually wears this - I could give it back to him - or her..."
"Yeah weird. But I think that belongs to Tom."
"Tom? Oh does he live around here? I could quickly drop it off now if.."
"No, Tom, our barista Tom. I'll just grab him."
Still reeling that hot barista guy is called Tom, I didn't even realise what that meant until Tom come around to the till.
"Hey! Oh, you found my mask!"
"Your..it's yours?"
"Yeah, I know it looks a bit funny, but my mum hand made it for me haha."
"That's so nice of her!" I whispered, still trying to comprehend what he was telling me.
"Ah, she worries. But I am definitely glad I don't have to tell her I lost it, so thanks for that."

I smiled up at him, not sure what the fuck to say. I couldn't help but stare at him as I went through my mental checklist. Tall, short black hair, mask with red straps. Was he Mystery Window Boy? I knew Window Boy all of this time?

"Hey, let me buy you coffee - from somewhere nicer, when I'm not working, to say thank you."

"That would be nice! I'm Sam by the way."

"Sam." He whispered. I swear the smile he gave me almost made my knees give out.

As I left the cafe, I turned to look back at Tom, and he says "I almost forgot to mention, you should read..."

And then I woke up.

Haha just kidding!! But holy shit did it feel like a dream!

To: Sam.Duffy@aol.com

From: Richards.Sally@London.ac.uk

Subject: Your progress so far

Hi Samantha,

It has been lovely getting to know you through your diary entries this past year. As you might be aware, it is up to myself to deem whether you should continue with daily diary entries or commence them all together.

This past year has been very difficult and trying for so many of us, and yet I have been amazed at your progress. I hope that you continue with the habit of writing down your feelings in the future. In saying this, I am happy to let you know, that as of this afternoon, in an official statement from The University of London, you have been acquitted of the damages you have cost the University and are no longer required to write daily diary entries.

Wishing you the best of luck.

Kind Regards,
Dr Sally Richards.

Journal of Sam Duffy

Day 251

My last entry....
What can I say Dr Richards, except I'm grateful for your advice. I think the diary entries really helped me to sort out my feelings and notice my unhealthy thinking patterns. I also love that I have this sort of book, that I have documented my whole relationship beginnings, so I will never forget how I met Tom and what I was like before him.

The thing I have come to learn is that if you are with someone who doesn't make you feel beautiful - no matter how you may look or think you look - then you are most definitely with the wrong guy. I never feel self-conscious around him, I just feel safe.

And you know what else! I was right - Martin was Walter to my Meg Ryan. There was no magic! Didn't even know what that meant until now.

God, sorry you probably don't want to hear about me swooning over my boyfriend!

....well I'm going to do it anyway!

He is now part of my bubble! Aka Tom and I are moving in together!!

Or he is moving in with me. Mia and Parker love Tom, so they were stoked when I told them. I know it's only been like three months, and the UK is about to go back into lockdown, but I have never ever been more sure of this in my life. When I moved in with Walter - I mean Martin haha - it was like a convenience thing, instead of what it is now. I just want to be around Tom all the time!

And don't worry, I will be fine! I have decided to keep writing every day, as well. But maybe in a new, prettier diary that doesn't remind me of being dumped and almost arrested in one day.

Sam x

P.s you should date a barista Dr R! Free, amazing coffee every morning. It's like heaven :)

Acknowledgements

Thank you to my sister and mum for re-reading every single chapter change, and dealing with my self-conscious ramblings during the writing process. And lastly, thank you to Nick, and my whole family for believing in me. This book would have stayed a scribbled note hoarded in a draw somewhere without your support.

Also by Caroline Carter

SPY VS ASSASSIN

Some say she is soulless. Others claim her heart is as black as a moonless night. Between the legend and rumor, one fact is known: at just 24, Nadia is the most ruthless assassin in the Institute's arsenal. No man is beyond her reach.

When a new hit is ordered, Nadia must carefully mask her surprise. She has no qualms killing a pair of brothers she's never met, but why would the Institute send their deadliest weapon to do a job their janitor could manage? Something is off.

Things grow even stranger when a coded message appears from a long-lost friend. A friend who once meant everything to Nadia, before they disappeared. But friendship is for civilians not assassins, and hope is a vulnerability she cannot afford.

Right or wrong, Nadia is caught in a web of deceit and destruction and for the first time in her short life, the lethal spider might have become the fly.

Made in the USA
Monee, IL
13 November 2020